And I Lo⟩

CW00498780

To Ann

Best Wishes.

Chris Mowatt

Chris Mowatt

Table of Contents

Dedication

For Margaret, Paul and Andy

Acknowledgement

Thanks to Andy, Nataliya, Lynda, Dawn, Janet and Lynette, who read my manuscript and offered encouragement.

Thanks to John Lennon and Paul McCartney, who, unknowingly with their song, provided the title for the book.

About the Author

Chris was born in Manchester and raised in East Manchester. He attended a primary school in Droylsden and then Audenshaw Grammar School. When he was about 13, his family moved to Southport. So, he continued his education at King George V Grammar School Southport and later at St Paul's College Cheltenham.

Chris qualified as a teacher and later gained an Advanced Diploma in Children's Literature. After leaving college, he was appointed to a teaching post in a local primary school and worked there for 38 years, spending 23 of those years as the deputy head.

Chris' main hobby is photography, and he is a member of two local camera clubs. He enjoys entering competitions and exhibitions, and his images get accepted in exhibitions all over the world. Not just that, Chris is a die-hard Manchester City FC fan. He has supported the club since childhood, and, having a season ticket, he has hardly missed a home game in the last twenty years.

Chris is happily married with two grown-up sons.

Chapter: 1

Cameron was in Brussels. The photoshoot the previous day had gone really well. He was extremely pleased with the results and so, apparently, was the client, as he had included a bonus on top of the agreed fee, which was to be added to the final payment. Before driving back to Calais to catch Le Shuttle, he decided to take a walk around La Grande Place. It was a lovely warm, late spring, early summer morning, and so just for a change, he decided to take some photographs for his own use, as some parts of the buildings around the square reminded him a little of the rather grand Victorian Town Hall back home. He spent a happy half hour or so just clicking away, and having done that, he realised that he had time for a coffee and sat at one of the outside tables to watch the world go by. He was just finishing his coffee and thinking of leaving when he was startled by a voice.

"Cameron Mason! What on earth are you doing here?"

He looked up and was shocked to see Penny, older, of course, but just as attractive as he remembered her. She had a little girl with her, no more than two or three years old.

He stood up. "I might ask you the same question," he replied with a smile.

"I live here, remember," she answered with a grin as she gave him a peck on the cheek. They both sat down. She repeated her question. "So, what are you doing here?"

"Actually, I was here on business, and if you hadn't turned up. I was about to leave. And, who's this?" he said, looking at the toddler, who was acting rather shyly and clinging on to her mum's leg.

"This is Maisie. Maisie say 'Bonjour' to Cameron." Maisie responded with a very quiet 'Bonjour'.

"She's lovely, Penny. You are married then?"

"No, Cameron. Sadly I'm not. I thought that I was going to be married," she replied wistfully, "but it turned out that I was just his little dalliance. Maisie was the result, but she's gorgeous, and I love her. So do mum and dad. They dote on her, and she's spoilt terribly. It doesn't help that we live in the same house. We have our own flat, though, but it does mean that we do see rather a lot of grandma and grandpa. Anyway, enough about me, why are you here?"

"Like I said. Business. I am a professional commercial photographer now, and the big hotel around the corner, which has just been refurbished, hired me to do the publicity shots for its new brochure. It's part of a chain of hotels. I work for them quite often. I do a lot of that kind of work all over western Europe."

She looked at him with a puzzled expression. "No chemistry, then?" He shook his head.

"No chemistry," he laughed. "I got into photography by chance and loved it."

She looked at him, "And tell me, Cameron, how is Coral?" He didn't answer. He found himself looking at the floor.

She noticed that. She raised her voice a little, "Cameron, look at me." He looked up at her. She could see the sadness in his eyes.

She asked him again. "How is Coral?"

"I honestly don't know," he replied.

"What do you mean, you don't know?"

"We've sort of lost touch."

She almost shouted at him, "Cameron, you idiot, how could you lose touch with her? She was the love of your life. She still is. I can see it in your eyes. How did this happen?"

"I don't really know. It just sort of happened when we were at university. No mobile phones or emails back then. She was at Edinburgh. I went to Exeter. We couldn't have been further apart."

"Has there been anyone else?" she asked.

3

He shook his head. "I've had a few friends, but never another girlfriend. There was one that tried to get close, but I pushed her away just like I did with you."

She looked at him. "Cameron, get back up to the north of England and find her again." There was a silence. "I mean it, Cameron, go and find her."

He looked at her, "I daren't, Penny."

"Why ever not?"

"I'm scared that she might have found someone else. While I don't know, I can cope, but if she had found someone else..." His voice tailed off, and he looked away.

"Cameron, look at me." He looked at her. "Cameron, get back to England and find her. Believe me. Coral will not have found someone else. I only met her a few times, but it was always you. It will always be you for her. Don't be stupid. Go and find her. Go straight up there tomorrow."

"I can't do that," he said sadly. "I'm shooting the stills for a shampoo commercial in London tomorrow."

"Go the next day then." She paused. "Cameron, promise me that you'll try and find her, and let me know when you do." She looked in her bag and handed him a business card. "Promise!"

He was looking at the card, "I promise," he said. Then he looked at the name over the coffee shop window, then at her card and then back at her. "This place is yours?"

She nodded. "It keeps me busy and out of mischief." She stood up, "I'll have to go in now; need to keep everyone on their toes. Come on, Maisie, say goodbye."

"Cameron, DO IT. And I expect to hear from you shortly." She kissed him on the cheek. "I'll sort this," she said, and she picked up the bill and went inside with Maisie.

As he drove to Calais, he thought about the things Penny had said. His feelings fluctuated. Sometimes he was elated as he thought that Coral would still be single. Other times, he was really down because he couldn't see how a lovely, pretty and intelligent girl like Coral would not have been whisked off by someone else. Some other lucky lad was bound to have taken his place. His mind was in a whirl, and he tried hard to push all thoughts of his conversation with Penny to the back of his mind and concentrate on his driving for the moment. Arriving in London, he checked into his hotel, had something to eat and then re-checked the brief for tomorrow's shoot.

Years earlier

They didn't call themselves 'The Gang': that was what the leaders of the youth club called them.

They were an extremely close-knit group of eight youngsters, in their early teens, within the youth club. Everyone agreed that it was unusual for youngsters of that age to be so close. It wasn't a deliberately exclusive group, and yet somehow, none of the other club members tried to intrude or join the group. An outsider visiting the youth club would not have realised that 'The Gang' existed at all. At the youth club meetings, every member of 'The Gang' always joined in with the club activities, easily paired up with other club members for games and generally had a good time with everyone.

And yet, when there was a lull or a bit of a break during the evening activities, there they were, in their corner, chatting and laughing away together.

The members of 'The Gang' had been in the same class at primary school, and it was there that this close bond was formed. They didn't know themselves how it had happened. At the time, they probably didn't realise that it had happened. It was just one of those things that occur from time to time. At the end of primary school, they were separated, and they went off to different secondary schools, but somehow the friendship wasn't broken, and they managed to stay together. That was partly down to Coral's parents and her mum in particular.

Coral's birthday was early in September, and one year, when they were planning her party, her mother had suggested that she invited some of her old friends from primary school. Coral jumped at the idea and knew exactly who she wanted at her party. She invited just seven old friends. She sat down to write the invitations. Six of the letters were exactly the same.

Dear...,

Please come to my party on Saturday 20th September at 4.30 pm.

From,

Coral.

The seventh letter was slightly different.

Dear Cameron,

Please come to my party on Saturday 20th September at 4.30 pm

Love from Coral xxx

Mrs Browne noticed the slight difference and half made a mental note. Cameron only lived a few doors away and had always been friendly with Coral.

When their children were at primary school, Mrs Browne and Mrs Mason often walked to school together with the

7

children and sometimes, when the need arose, one of them would happily collect both children and bring them home. It was not unusual to find the two of them playing in the other's garden.

Coral was really pleased when they all accepted the invitations. The replies came back very quickly. There were four boys and three girls, but the acceptance that excited Coral the most was Cameron's. She waved it at her mum. "Cameron is coming as well," she almost shouted.

"Did you ever think that he wouldn't?" Her mum replied with a smile.

Chapter: 2

Party day arrived, and Coral could hardly wait. She was hopping around with excitement and dashed to the door every time the bell rang. She only really settled when Cameron arrived. She thanked him for the little present and the card. Mrs Browne noticed that Coral made sure that his card was the most prominent of all.

The party was a huge success, and Coral's mum was impressed with the way the youngsters all got on together and were comfortable in the company of each other. They circulated. The boys didn't sit in one corner and the girls in another. They mixed freely and joined in the party games. They laughed a lot with each other, not at each other and had a really good time. Mrs Browne was both surprised and delighted to see that they all appeared to have manners. No one pushed to get at the food on the table.

Buffet time was about the only time there was any semblance of quiet. No food ended up on the floor, and no one filled their plate and then didn't eat what was on it. She noted that when it was time to leave, every one of them went to Coral and said, "Thank you for the invitation," or something similar to that, and as a group, they came to Mrs Browne and said goodbye and thanked her for putting up with them. They apologised if it had got a bit too noisy.

"All I could hear was lots of laughter," she said.

Right after that party, she decided that she was going to nurture this group. From that day on, it was an open house at the Browne's on a Friday evening and 'The Gang' was well and truly formed.

It was even better when the youth club started and 'The Gang' decided to join. That took care of Saturday night as well. The youth club was a new venture for the community and was something that was sorely needed. It met in the local church hall. It turned out to be a success which, in no small part, was down to the enthusiasm of 'The Gang'.

There had not been a great deal to do before the youth club, but the boys did play in the same football team, and their team was quite successful. If it wasn't too cold on Saturday mornings in winter and the team was playing at home, the girls would, more often than not, turn up to support their friends. Apart from a few parents, they were usually the only four people on the touchline.

When summer arrived, the youth club ceased to meet formally, but most of the members could then usually be found in the park. They would arrive in dribs and drabs and join in the ad hoc games of rounders, cricket, and football or perhaps just kick or lob a ball around. Anyone was free to join in, and they usually did, but as the games drew to a natural close, and the night started to fall, 'The Gang' would often end up sitting in a circle on the grass just chatting, and somehow those who had joined in the games knew that at this point, it was probably time to say good night and leave them to it.

As darkness fell, the group would all leave together, only splitting up as they went their separate ways, the numbers getting smaller as one by one they peeled off to their own homes, and then just Coral and Cameron were left together and then just Cameron.

One evening after the games were finished, it started to get a little windy, and they decided to leave. Gordon noticed that the ball had started to roll away, and with the wind catching it, it was gathering speed.

"I'll get it," he said. He got up and dashed after it. No one knows to this day how it happened, but somehow he tripped and fell.

There was an extremely loud snapping noise as he landed, and the scream that followed was earth-shattering.

Cameron and Coral reached him first, followed by Ian and Pam. Coral took one look at his misshapen arm, turned as white as a sheet, stumbled away and threw up on the grass. The next few minutes were a bit of a haze. Tony lived nearest to the park, so he ran home to get his mum to ring for an ambulance. Ian and Pam did their best to look after Gordon. Jenny and Kate ran to Gordon's house to get his mum or dad.

Cameron found himself looking after Coral. He had his arms around her as she leaned into his chest, muttering, "It's horrible, it's horrible, poor Gordon," and she was sobbing quietly. All the while, Cameron could hear Gordon crying in pain and then looking towards him, he could see him starting to shake.

He gently sat Coral on the grass. "Just sit here, Coral, while I see to Gordon." He took off his zipper jacket and tried to wrap it around Gordon.

"We've got to try and keep him warm. He's going into shock," he told Ian and Pam. Ian took off his jacket as well and wrapped it around Gordon as best he could.

Suddenly there were adults everywhere. Tony's mum and Tony arrived. She had a blanket.

"The ambulance is on its way," she said.

Gordon's dad appeared, followed by Jenny and Kate. He went straight to Gordon, who by this time was a little calmer and tried to lighten the mood.

"You clumsy oaf," he said, "How did you manage to do this?"

It didn't help matters much, but then the ambulance arrived, and some sort of order was restored. Cameron retrieved his jacket and went back to Coral, put it over her shoulders and then sat with his arm around her.

As the ambulance crew were leaving with Gordon and his dad, one of the crew turned to them and said, "You youngsters did alright tonight, you did all the right things…well done…and especially you." He pointed his finger straight at Cameron, "From what I've gathered, you sorted everything."

Cameron looked puzzled. "Me! I didn't do anything."

"That's not what your friends here are telling me. I asked what had happened, and they said that you organised them all. Well done." With that, the ambulance crew, Gordon and his dad, were off.

"He's right Cam," said Ian. "You did sort it. You sent Tony off home. You sent Jenny and Kate to get Gordon's dad. You told Pam and me to stay with him and try and calm him. Don't you remember?"

"Not really. Everything was just a bit of a blur. I just knew things needed to be sorted."

Coral smiled and looked up at him. "And you looked after me."

Cameron looked a bit embarrassed. "I didn't mean to boss you around. I just sort of did it."

By now, they were strolling to the park gate.

"Well, it's a good job that someone knew what to do," Jenny remarked, "but you've forgotten one thing."

"What's that?" Cameron asked.

"The ball," she replied. There was a slight pause, and then for the first time in an hour or so, they all laughed and headed home.

In the end, Cameron and Coral were left to walk on together.

They were subdued, and the chat didn't flow as it usually did. Suddenly Coral stopped.

"Cameron...will you put your arm around me again? It felt nice when you did it before." Without answering, he reached out and pulled her to him. They walked on again with her head resting on his shoulder. When they reached her gate, he made to go on as he normally did, but she grabbed his hand and pulled him up the path.

He looked at her with a puzzled expression, "What's going on."

By now, they were at her front door, and she had opened it. "Mum."

Mrs Browne appeared. "Hello love, hello Cameron."

Coral recounted the whole story leaving nothing out. Not even the sick! She took special pains to explain how Cameron had looked after her as well as organising the others.

"It seems to me that you've done very well tonight, Cameron, and thank you for looking after Coral. But it doesn't really surprise me. You are a good lad." She turned away. "I'll leave you two to say good night," and she disappeared down the hallway.

When she was out of sight, Coral looked at Cameron. "Thank you for looking after me."

"That's okay. It was nothing. We're friends, aren't we?" he smiled. She was still looking at him, but it was a slightly different look than the ones she usually gave him.

"What!"

She reached up and pulled his face towards her, and kissed him.

It was the first time he had ever been kissed by anyone other than his mum.

There was a slight pause as he looked into her eyes, and then he kissed her back.

They drew away from each other and smiled.

"That was a surprise," said Cameron, "but nice." He kissed her again.

A voice from inside shouted, "When you two have quite finished, it's time to come in, Coral."

"Yes, mum...Coming." She kissed him again. "See you tomorrow."

When she had gone inside with a final wave, he stood for a few moments before turning to walk up the path, shutting the gate and heading home. All in all, it had been an interesting evening.

Chapter: 3

At school the next day, Cameron found it hard to concentrate. In the science lesson, he was brought up short by Miss Baxter.

"Cameron! Are you paying attention? You don't seem to be with us today. It's not like you. Is anything wrong?"

It wasn't like him. He enjoyed school most of the time and especially science. Partly because he found it interesting and, he had to admit, partly because of Miss Baxter. Not only was she a good teacher, but she was also very attractive, and most of his classmates were secretly in love with her.

He had been hooked on science since the very first lesson in the first week of year 7. It was a year lecture and the whole of year 7 were in the main hall. On the stage, dressed in a white lab coat, and darting about all over the place, conducting fascinating experiments, was one of the senior science teachers. He was almost the embodiment of a mad professor. The trick that stuck in Cameron's mind was hammering a nail into a piece of wood with a sausage.

The teacher fastened the sausage to a piece of wood to make a hammer shape. Then he dipped the sausage end into a silver-coloured container that looked as if it had steam coming out of it. (He knew now that it was liquid nitrogen.) When the sausage was lifted out, it was frozen solid, and the teacher promptly used it to hammer the nail into the wood. To Cameron, this was fascinating, and it was like opening the door to a hidden world that he wanted to explore.

"Sorry, Miss. Just a bit upset. In the park last night, one of my friends tripped and fell. We heard his arm snap, and when we got to him, it looked as if he had two elbows on the same arm." At this, there were gasps and moans of disgust from the rest of the class. "I was just thinking about it. Sorry miss."

"That's awful, Cameron but do try and concentrate, please."

"Yes, miss, sorry Miss."

But if the truth be known, that wasn't all he was thinking about. There was this kissing thing with Coral. It was unexpected. They were friends, granted, and they had known each other for years, but he had never considered the boyfriend/girlfriend situation. Now that it seemed as though it might be happening, he quite liked the idea.

Coral was pretty. He knew that. It had never really been relevant before. She was clever. She wanted to be a vet. She was funny and almost always smiling. The more he thought about it, the more he liked it.

When the lesson was over, Miss Baxter stopped him as he was leaving the lab. "Are you sure that you are alright, Cameron? There is such a thing as delayed shock, you know."

"I'm fine, miss, honestly."

"Is your friend a pupil here?"

"No, Miss. He goes to Moss Side."

"Well, be sure to check on him and let me know how he is getting on."

"Yes, Miss."

Later at lunch, he had to field all sorts of questions from some of his friends. He had to describe the gory details. How loud was the scream? What did his arm look like? Did you feel sick when you saw it?

He was about to say, "No, but Coral actually was sick," but thought better of it. Coral, he decided, was someone that he wanted to keep to himself.

On his way home, he stopped by Gordon's.

His mum answered the door. "Cameron, it's lovely to see you. Thank you for looking after Gordon and sorting things last night. You did a good job. Everyone thinks that you did all the right things."

"We were all there. We all helped," he said, feeling a little uncomfortable. "How is he?"

"They are keeping him overnight. He's had an operation today. One of the bones needed a plate. But he's going to be fine. We are going to see him later."

"Okay. That's good then. Tell him I called."

With that, he turned to go.

"Cameron." He turned back. "Thank you."

When he got home, his mum asked if he'd been to see Gordon.

"Yes, but he's still in the hospital. He's had to have an operation to mend the bone, but he's okay. His mum and dad are going to see him tonight."

There was some homework to do, then tea and then the homework to finish. He was just checking it over for the final time when the doorbell rang. He heard his mum open the door, some quiet voices and then.

"Cameron, it's someone to see you."

"Coming." He gathered his things together and put them in his bag for the morning.

Coral was at the door. She looked a little sheepish.

He was pleased to see her. "Hi. Are you okay?"

"It's about last night."

"Yes." He smiled. "Which bit of last night are you thinking about?"

"You know very well which bit, and you are laughing at me."

"No, I'm not. Come on." He grabbed her hand and headed out of the door shouting, "Mum, we're just off out. Won't be long."

He kept hold of her hand even while he was shutting the gate, and they walked down the street hand in hand for the very first time.

They headed towards the canal towpath.

"If you were talking about the kissing on your doorstep, I've been thinking about it all day. It was the best bit of last night, even if it nearly did get me into trouble in science. We've been friends for ages, but suddenly last night, it was different even before the kissing. I liked holding you close while you recovered from spewing up."

"Do you really mean that?"

"Yes," and he let go of her hand and put his arm around her shoulder. She leaned in to him just as she had done last

21

night. By now, they were approaching the canal bridge. When they were underneath, they stopped. He looked at her and said, "Shall we try it again?"

"What, the holding or the kissing?"

"Both," he said.

She looked up at him and nodded. So they did.

In bed that night, he thought a lot about the last few days. He realised that things would change. He liked Coral a lot, and after tonight he knew that she liked him too. She even told him that she had wanted to kiss him for ages but was scared in case it spoilt their friendship and put him off. She'd rather have him as just a friend than not a friend at all. Well, that was settled now. As far as they were concerned, they were together, and at the moment, it felt good. His slight worry was how the others would react.

Later in the week, he saw Miss Baxter. "My friend is home now, he told her. His arm is in a cast, and he has to wear a sling."

"Was it his left or right arm that he broke?"

"His right, miss."

"Oh, dear…That's unfortunate school wise."

"No, it's not Miss," he chuckled, "He's left-handed." She looked at him for a split second, and then they both laughed.

"How unlucky is that?" she said, "See you in science tomorrow."

When the Youth club restarted in the autumn after Gordon's accident, the youth leaders, in particular, noticed a subtle difference in 'The Gang'. They seemed more grown-up, more responsible. They were almost always first at the club to help set things up: last to leave after helping tidy up. They took care of the younger members and the new members. They made them feel welcome and seemed to be able to act as arbiters in petty differences, and yet they were still 'The Gang'.

They also put ideas to the leaders, one of which was that perhaps, following Gordon's accident, there should be a First Aid Class as part of an evening, maybe once or twice a month. The suggestion was readily accepted, and so twice a month, members of St John's Ambulance Brigade came and taught First Aid for half an hour.

Even though it was serious, all the club members enjoyed it and had great fun learning how to make slings or tie bandages. The first few attempts were disastrous and caused howls of laughter, but in the end, they started to get the hang of it. Some of them also had doubts about mouth to mouth

23

procedures. They liked their friends but weren't too sure about getting so close up to them, so a dummy appeared after that to solve the problem.

Since the accident, it was now clear to the others that Cameron and Coral were together, and there seemed to be a growing affection between Ian and Pam. The rest of the group didn't seem to mind. In fact, Jenny and Kate wondered why it had taken Cameron and Coral so long 'to get together' as they put it. It had been obvious for ages that they were mad about each other. When they said as much to Tony and Gordon, Tony replied that he had never noticed any such thing.

"That's because you're a boy then," they said.

"Oh. Good, you've noticed," he said, laughing.

As for the meetings at the Browne's house, they continued as normal. Sometimes Mrs Browne arranged outings for them. She would book them in at the Bowling Alley or the Ice Rink. The first time they went skating, Kate laughingly said to Gordon, "You take care. You fall over on grass! There's no telling what will happen when you get on the ice."

"I'll try hard to stay on my feet," he replied, smiling at her. Everyone joined in.

"Yes, you be careful."

They needn't have worried. It turned out that Gordon was a natural on ice, far better than any of the others. He enjoyed it so much that later, he started having lessons.

With Christmas approaching, Mr and Mrs Browne realised that Coral would expect Cameron to be included in at least some of their family celebrations. Mrs Browne visited Cameron's mum towards the beginning of December and explained what they had been thinking.

Mrs Mason waited until she had finished and then replied, "Snap, we were thinking of inviting Coral to some of ours. We weren't sure how you would take it."

"I know they do see an awful lot of each other, and they are very young, but our Coral is really happy at the moment. I think that she would be extremely disappointed if she couldn't see Cameron over Christmas."

Chapter: 4

Mrs Mason had to admit that she thought that Cameron would also be disappointed. So an arrangement was reached. On Christmas Day, the youngsters could visit each other's house for an hour or two.

Before Christmas arrived, though, there was the Youth Club party to organise. 'The Gang' were fully involved. They decorated the hall with tinsel, streamers and balloons, planned the games and helped in the kitchen to get the food ready.

"There's no mistletoe," someone remarked.

"That won't matter to Coral and Cameron," Tony joked.

About halfway through the evening, Tony said to Cameron, "Cam, I could do with a little help here. Come on."

Cameron looked a bit puzzled but stood up and followed him to one of the side rooms. Inside, there was a musical keyboard on its stand. Cameron looked at Tony.

"Yours?"

"Yes, come on, let's get it set up."

He picked up the keyboard and went back into the main hall. Cameron trailed behind with the stand. They set it up by the Christmas Tree. Tony found a chair, and whilst everyone else was having something to eat, he played a medley of Christmas songs. When he had finished and started to walk back to the Gang Corner, the whole room started clapping and cheering. He did a mock bow coupled with a slightly embarrassed smile.

"We didn't know you could play the keyboard," Kate remarked when he reached them.

"Well, not everyone knows everything about everybody," was his reply. "Jenny could be good at knitting, Pam good at drawing, or Ian could collect stamps for all I know."

Jane, one of the leaders, came across. "That was lovely, Tony. We were wondering, can you play any carols? We thought it might be nice to end with a bit of carol singing."

"If you can find the music, I will probably be able to play them."

"You didn't use music before," Jane pointed out.

"No, but I need the music at first and then after I have played it a few times, I can remember it somehow. We'll need some words as well."

"This is a church hall, Tony. I am pretty sure that we should be able to find a few hymn books and the music to go with them," Jane replied laughingly.

The party went really well, and everyone had a great time. "Not one little melodrama all evening," remarked Gordon's mum, who had volunteered to help out. In addition, the leaders noted that Ian and Pam were now definitely very close now, whilst Tony and Kate also seemed to get on really well together. John, one of the leaders, reported that he had noticed that Tony and Kate hadn't let the absence of mistletoe be much of a hindrance to their enjoyment!

To finish off, they gathered around the Christmas Tree to sing carols. They sang a few well-known ones with the help of the hymn books. It went better than any of the adults had expected, and Jane noticed that several of them had rather good voices.

Finally, she said, "It would be nice if we could finish with 'Away in a manger, but the first verse is usually a solo."

"I'll do the solo," offered Annie, much to everyone's surprise. Annie was one of the quietest members of the club. Jane never flinched. "Okay, Annie, you sing the solo. Off we go, Tony."

The second Annie sang the first few words, stunned expressions crossed the faces of almost everyone. She sang beautifully. When she had finished, there was a brief silence, then Jenny said, "I'm not sure whether it's right to clap after

28

a carol, but I'm going to anyway. That was lovely, Annie." She clapped her, and the rest joined in.

"That was a surprise, Annie. We never knew that you could sing like that. It really was lovely," smiled Jane.

"Like I said earlier," Tony chimed in. "Not everyone knows everything about everybody."

"That's true," said Jane, "Now, should we sing the whole carol? Annie can sing the first verse again, and everyone can join in with the second and third verse." So they did.

On Christmas Day, Coral and Cameron did get to spend time with each other and exchange presents. Coral had recently had her ears pierced. Cameron had enlisted his mum's help to choose a set of earrings. His mum had also wrapped the box and put a Christmas Bow on it. Coral's eyes lit up when she opened it. "They are so nice," she smiled, "Thank you, I love them."

Later, Cameron's dad reckoned that if Cameron had only given her a chocolate bar, she would have been just as pleased.

For her part, she gave Cameron a real silver biro in a box. "It's so every time you use it, you'll think of me," she laughed.

Christmas passed, and New Year came. Tony's mum invited 'The Gang' around on New Year's Eve. They had a great time and made Tony play his keyboard. It turned out that he could play virtually anything from The Beatles to Beethoven. Much to their surprise, they spent quite a lot of time singing along, especially to the more well-known songs, most of which seemed to come from the 60s.

Towards the end of the holidays, there was one bit of news that did upset them. They heard that James, one of the younger boys in the club, had been attacked by a couple of older boys and had his watch stolen. The watch had been a Christmas present.

"Right," said Ian. "When the club starts up again, we will ask if they can arrange some self-defence classes." Everyone agreed that that was a great idea. The Club leaders thought so too.

John knew a martial arts expert who agreed to help out, and so self-defence classes started early in January. They happened an hour before the proper meeting time so that those that weren't interested didn't miss club time.

In the event, it turned out that nearly all the members turned up anyway, boys and girls, probably in part, encouraged by parents who had heard about James's misfortune.

Meanwhile, Jane had been impressed with the carol singing at the party, and the seeds of an idea were forming in her head. She had recently heard the young people's version of 'Joseph and the Amazing Technicolour Dreamcoat', and she began to wonder if the Youth Club would like to try to perform it.

At a meeting towards the beginning of February, she got them all to sit down and put the idea to them. "Before you answer, let's listen to it," she said. She also passed the words around so that they knew exactly what was being sung. It went better than she expected. When the recording was finished, she asked, "Well, what do you think?" She got a very positive response.

"There are some great tunes in this," Tony remarked, and they agreed to try it, but not before listening to it again, and this time they were able to join in a little. Tony was very enthusiastic. "I'll learn the tunes. I really like this music."

"There are some solos," Jane reminded them.

Jenny piped up, "Annie can sing them."

"Maybe," Jane replied, "but we will need more than one soloist."

Rehearsals were held during the normal Saturday evening meetings, and so as not to make it too much like hard work, they only lasted twenty minutes or so. Tony was as good as his word, and within three weeks, he had mastered all the tunes. In the end, the soloists picked themselves. Annie, of course, and James turned out to be the surprise package. Everyone was pleased because ever since the incident after Christmas, he seemed to have lost his confidence and had been a bit withdrawn. As the rehearsals progressed, it was obvious that James was enjoying himself, and he was beginning to be more like his old self.

It was decided that they would give the performance at the beginning of April. The church hall needed decorating, so they decided that all the profits would go to the Decoration Fund. Tickets were printed and then sold to friends and families. Posters were created. It turned out that Pam was very good at graphic design. The posters that she produced looked almost professional.

"See," said Tony, "I was right. We never knew that Pam could do stuff like this. They're great."

They realised that the performance of 'Joseph' would not fill the whole evening, so they learnt some well-known songs that everybody could join in with, and had some song sheets printed. A few of the mums volunteered to help with the refreshments. As the day drew closer, some of the youngsters began to wonder if anybody would actually turn up.

As it happened, they needn't have worried. The hall was packed with not a spare seat anywhere. 'Joseph' was the first half of the evening.

As James finished the last notes of 'Any Dream Will Do', there was a split second of stunned silence and then a tremendous round of applause. Some of the audience stood up to applaud, and they were quickly followed by most of the rest of the audience. When the applause had finished, Jane thanked the slightly embarrassed youngsters for their hard work and announced the refreshments. The second half of the evening went equally as well, with everyone enjoying the singalong. After the final song, there was a bit of a surprise.

The vicar strode onto the stage and thanked them. "I am sure that you will agree that this has been an excellent evening. We never knew that we had such talent in our Youth Club. I have got two requests."

"Firstly, it seems such a shame that after all your hard work that you perform 'Joseph' only once. Can I persuade you to do it again in church a week on Sunday? Secondly, before we all go home, can I persuade James to sing 'Any Dream Will Do' again? I am sure that we would all love to hear it again, wouldn't we?"

This was greeted by shouts of approval. A slightly reluctant James was ushered to the front of the stage. However, as Tony played the introduction, he became full of confidence again and sang it beautifully. When he had finished, the applause was just as loud, if not louder than before.

The vicar got his wish, and they performed 'Joseph' in church the following Sunday. He apologised to the congregation, which was a good deal larger than usual, that the service would not follow the normal format. "A lot of us were thrilled last week by the performance of the Youth Club, and if you didn't see it, you missed a wonderful evening. It was too good to do it only once, so they are going to repeat it again this morning. I can assure you that you are in for a treat."

In the end, even though they were in church, the congregation clapped loudly and enthusiastically. When the applause died down, the vicar stood up and said, "What did I tell you; wasn't that wonderful? I expect many of you will be humming the tunes for days to come." He turned to the youngsters and thanked them for their excellent contribution to the service.

When the service was over, many of the congregation made a point of approaching the teenagers and thanking them for their contribution. Some of them could be heard outside, telling them, 'It was lovely' or 'that was wonderful' as they left the church.

Meanwhile, 'The Gang' continued to meet on a Friday at the Browne's and occasionally on a Sunday evening at Tony's house or Pam's house. Seemingly, all the parents were happy to allow their offspring to get together so often.

"It's amazing how well they all get on," Pam's mum remarked to Mrs Browne when they bumped into each other one afternoon. Mrs Browne agreed but admitted she was surprised how well the friendships had lasted. The only thing she wasn't surprised about was Coral and Cameron.

"They are made for each other," she said.

Indeed, Coral and Cameron were almost inseparable. Hardly a day went by when they didn't meet up for at least half an hour in one house or the other.

One evening, his dad came up to his room. "Are you busy, Cam?"

"Just finishing maths homework, dad, then I'm off to see Coral. She wants a bit of help with some science."

"It's about Coral. Now, I don't want you to take this the wrong way. She's a lovely girl, and your mum and I really like her, but don't let her get in the way of your schoolwork.

35

You are both very young, and you are seeing rather a lot of each other at the moment."

Cameron looked at his dad. "Dad, I know this sounds a bit grown up, but she makes me happy, and if anything, my grades have got better since we really got together. Look!"

He produced two or three of his books from his rucksack and handed them to his dad, who sat down on the bed and flicked through them. Finally, he put them down. "Those are good, Cameron. I'm pleased, but just keep in mind what I said."

"Yes, dad."

It was true things were going well at school. Most of the time, he found the work fairly easy. It was just French that he found a little confusing. There were two words for 'you', two words for 'the' and two words for 'a'. What was all that about? And how could 'la fenetre' (the window) be feminine?

Chapter: 5

Cameron enjoyed all sport and very early in the summer term, he had been picked for the 'Under 15 Cricket Team', which played against other schools on a Wednesday afternoon. He was 15 now, but to play for the U15s, you had to be under 15 at the start of the school year.

He had done well with bat and ball in several matches, and after one game, the PE teacher, Mr Davis, asked him if he fancied joining the Canalside Cricket Club and playing for their U16 team. "They practise on Mondays and play on Tuesdays," Mr Davis told him.

"I'll think about it, sir. I'll have to talk to my dad about it," and Coral too, he thought.

It turned out that his dad was quite happy with it, as long as it didn't interfere with school work. "I used to play a bit myself," he said.

Coral said he should do it because he enjoyed it, and if he didn't do it because of her, he might regret it one day and blame her.

He joined the Canalside Cricket Club, and on quite a few Tuesday evenings, two people sat side by side to watch him play; His dad and Coral. After the games were over, his dad would tactfully leave to let them walk home together.

The summer exams were over, and Cameron knew that he had done well. When the results came out, he was in the top four for everything and the very top for science. Even in French, he was surprised to find that he came tenth. His parents were delighted the day he brought his report home.

"We are really pleased, Cameron, aren't we?" His mum said. She turned to look at his dad.

"Really good, Cameron, really good," was all he said as he sat quietly looking at the report. Then he looked up and smiled, "Really good," he said again.

After tea, he went to see Coral. Mr and Mrs Browne let them use their front room to sit and talk, play music, watch TV and sometimes help each other with homework. Coral's mum asked how the exams had gone.

"Very well," he replied. "Mum and dad seem pleased."

"That's both of you then." He knew that Coral's results were good because she had rushed round to tell him the day before.

He had just got back home when there was a knock at the door. He went to open it and was slightly surprised to see Mrs Browne."

"Hi Cameron, is your mum or dad in?"

"Both are," he said. "Mum, dad. It's Mrs Browne for you. Come in, Mrs Browne," and he showed her through to the living room.

She turned to Cameron and said, "Do you mind if I have a word with them in private, Cameron."

"No, Mrs Browne, but you've got me worried. Have I done something wrong?"

"Not at all, love. You've got nothing to worry about."

"Thank goodness for that," and he left the room.

He was intrigued. He could hear them talking, no raised voices. That was a good sign. He was sitting reading the paper in the front room when the door opened, and Mrs Browne came in, followed by his mum.

Mrs Browne spoke. "Cameron, there is something I would like to ask you." She paused. "We, the three of us, that's me, Coral's dad and Coral, have booked a gite in France for a fortnight. Do you know what a gite is?"

"Yes, it's a sort of holiday cottage."

"That's right. Well, we were wondering if you would like to come with us?"

There was a slight pause, which surprised the two women, and then he said, "Can I think about it?"

Then another long pause during which both women looked slightly puzzled. Then a few seconds later, "I've thought about it. Yes, please."

"Cameron! You are a bit of a tease," she smiled. "I think I know someone who will be very happy. In fact, I'm sure she will. Well, good night. I'll see you soon, and we can sort out the arrangements with your mum and dad," and then both women left the room.

"Good night Mrs Browne and thank you."

He sat down. "I wasn't expecting that," he thought to himself. However, he wasn't at all surprised, when five minutes later, there was a rather frantic knocking at the door. He went to open it, and she almost threw herself at him, gave him a kiss and said, "We are going to France together; won't that be great?"

Mrs Mason poked her head out of the living room door. "You seem happy, Coral love."

"Oh, I am, Mrs Mason. Thank you so much for letting him go with us."

His mum smiled, "Glad to get rid of him for two weeks. Now you'd better get back home. There's still school in the morning."

Chapter: 6

There was plenty to sort out over the next few weeks. For one thing, Cameron hadn't got a passport. To make sure that it came back in time, his dad drove to the passport office in Liverpool to deliver the application form in person. When it didn't arrive back within a few days, Coral got a bit panicky, but it turned up about a week before they were due to leave. His mum had also decided that he needed some new clothes, so a few trips to town had to be endured.

One evening, when they were in the front room at the Browne's, her dad came in and put a map on the floor.

"I thought that you might like to know where we are going." Cameron nodded. "Well, this is a map of Northern France, the bit called Normandy." He looked at Cameron. "Have you heard of it?"

Cameron nodded again and replied, "William the Conqueror came from there, and it's got a lot to do with D Day."

"That's right, and that's one of the reasons that we are going. My Uncle Bernard was killed in that battle, so we are going to visit his resting place. It's the 50th Anniversary of D Day this year. I hope you don't mind."

Cameron was really interested now. "Do you know where his grave is?"

"Yes, it's here, a little place called Ranville. It's not far from our cottage, which is here," and he pointed to another place. "It's called Asnelles, and it's right on the coast."

Cameron looked at the map for a few seconds and then said, "Asnelles is right next to Arromanches. That's where a lot of the troops landed on D Day."

"I'm impressed, Cameron. You are well informed."

"See, dad, he's not just a pretty face, and is that the end of the history lesson?"

"Yes, for now," her dad replied with a smile. "There might be some more later on," and leaving the map on the floor, he left them to it.

"How do you know about this stuff," she asked.

"There were programmes on the TV about it a few weeks back. I watched bits of them. It's interesting, though, and important."

They were booked on the early morning ferry from Portsmouth to Caen, so the car was loaded up during the previous late afternoon. "It gives us time to think about things that we might have forgotten," her dad said. Then just before 11.00 pm, they were off.

"Make sure you behave yourself, Cameron."

"Mum, don't worry, I will."

It was motorway most of the way. Cameron couldn't doze, but Coral did, occasionally coming to with a start and a question, "Where are we now?"

Just before 6.30 am, they arrived at the ferry terminal and checked in. Then all they had to do was wait to board.

"How are your sea legs, Cameron?" Mr Browne asked.

"Don't know, I guess I'll find out," was his reply. He needn't have worried.

"It looks as calm as a millpond," Mr Browne commented when they were settled in their lounge seats.

"It's almost a six-hour crossing, Cameron, so get some sleep if you can," said Mrs Browne.

But he couldn't sleep at first. Once they were underway, Coral and Cameron went to explore. They found the shop, and he bought two single-use cameras. They found the café and the slightly posher restaurant. When they got back to their seats, Coral delivered the expedition report. She took one of the cameras, gave it to her mum and said, "Take our picture, please," and she promptly sat on Cameron's lap with her head close to his and said, "Smile." He couldn't help it. He did.

Finally, Cameron did doze, but all the time, he was vaguely aware of things going on around him, and he knew that Coral was holding his hand. Later, he felt her let go of it and then heard quiet laughter. He opened his eyes just in time to see Coral put the camera down. "Did she just take a picture of me asleep?"

Still smiling, Mr and Mrs Browne nodded. Coral was still laughing, "Coral Browne, I'll get you back for that." She pulled a tongue at him, still laughing.

A while later, they noticed people moving to the lounge windows. In the far distance, on the horizon was a hazy grey line. France. It seemed to take ages to get closer, but then they started to make out features, and not much later, they were instructed to go to the car decks. It was mildly exciting to roll down the ramp and onto French soil.

"Remember to drive on the right," Mrs Browne prompted her husband. But he didn't need prompting. There were plenty of signs in English saying the same thing. "We need the road numbered 514. Keep your eyes peeled." They were waved through customs, and he didn't need their help as he turned right out of the docks onto the 514. The road followed the coast westwards through small towns with names like Luc-sur-Mer or Courseulles-sur-Mer. Cameron soon worked out that sur-Mer meant on the sea. His French wasn't wasted after all! Along the way, they passed plenty of war memorials, often in the form of tanks that were surrounded by allied flags fluttering in the gentle breeze.

He was fascinated.

"I didn't realise that there would be so many war items left around," he commented, "It's really interesting."

Coral looked at him a bit quizzically.

"What?" he asked. She shook her head. "Well, I think it is," he continued.

The adult Brownes chuckled. "Is this the first sign EVER of a disagreement between you two?" Mrs Browne asked.

Cameron and Coral looked at each other, "NO," they said in unison. Coral went on, "He's just never said he liked this sort of stuff before."

A short time later, they reached Asnelles and easily found the gite. It looked as if it had once been a barn, but now it was a very comfortable cottage. To Cameron, the inside looked as though it had all recently been decorated. There were three bedrooms upstairs, with the double having an en suite, and a large bathroom. Downstairs, there were two rooms plus a large kitchen.

"This all looks very nice," said Mr Browne, "Cameron, give us a hand with the luggage." The two of them unloaded the car whilst Coral and her mum put things away.

"A cup of tea now, I think," commented Mrs Browne.

While they were all sitting around, Mr Browne explained that probably they would not use the car again today. The journey started last night, and he had not had any proper sleep, and with having to remember to drive on the right, you needed all your wits about you. Lunch in a while and then perhaps a stroll to explore Asnelles was his suggestion.

So that's what they did. During the stroll, they found a small biscuit factory about 100 metres away from the gite.

"What does the notice say, Cameron?" asked Mrs Browne. He puzzled over it for a few seconds.

"It's open to visitors Monday to Friday 10.30 till 15.30, and that reminds me, have we altered our watches to French time?"

"Good point, Cameron," and Mr Browne immediately adjusted his watch.

"It also says they sell the biscuits in the shop from 9.00 am."

Not far away on the corner of the street, they found a memorial to the French Resistance and crossing the main road remembering to look LEFT first, they found a road no more than 50 metres long that led to the promenade and the beach. There were benches on the promenade, and they picked one and sat down.

Mrs Browne said, "You two can wander off if you want. You don't have to sit here with us." So they did. When they were a diplomatic distance away, they held hands. Mrs Browne, who had watched them go, smiled to herself. She was really fond of Cameron. She knew that Coral adored him, and although they were very young, she could see it lasting.

At the end of the promenade, they found a large concrete gun emplacement that once held a German heavy gun. You could see the slit where the barrel poked out. The concrete was pitted with shell and bullet holes. This made Coral start to take an interest. They tried to imagine what it must have been like inside when the battle was raging.

"Horrible, dangerous and frightening. Imagine seeing all those men coming ashore and knowing that they are going to try and kill you, and then knowing that you've got to shoot at them to save yourself," said Cameron.

They walked back the way they had come passing her mum and dad, still holding hands, and reported what they had found. Then they continued to the other end of the prom, where they found a similar gun emplacement. You could go into this one, but it wasn't very pleasant. "Dark and a bit eerie," Coral thought.

"It feels as though something really bad happened in here," she muttered, so they soon came out. There was an information plate on the side. Cameron read it as best he could.

"You were right. I think it says it was captured by the British on D Day, and three of the Germans inside were killed. It's not nice, but it was war."

To lighten the mood, they walked back along the beach. They decided to paddle as they walked, so trainers and socks came off. They stopped when they were almost level with her mum and dad. Suddenly, Coral threw her shoes as far as she could up the beach, kicked water at Cameron and ran off laughing. Cameron responded by dropping his shoes at the water's edge and chased after her.

They could hear her screaming. He soon caught her. She turned to face him, and he kissed her. She kissed him back. He looked her straight in the eyes, "Coral Browne, Will you marry me?"

She jumped up and down with excitement. "Yes, Yes, Yes." And she kissed him again.

Mr Browne turned to his wife, "They are very young. Do you really think it will last?"

"I do hope so," she replied, "Cameron is a lovely boy, and Coral will be devastated if it doesn't. It won't be her that finishes it if it doesn't last."

The two of them came running back up the beach, laughing and shoving each other. When they were close enough, Mrs Browne took a picture. It was only as she tried to take another that Coral noticed the camera, stopped and pulled Cameron closer to her and waved.

When they got back to the bench, Cameron laughingly said, "Look, Mrs Browne, Look what your daughter did to me. I'm soaked."

Coral said to her dad, "And he chased me."

"I didn't see you trying too hard to get away, love," was his response. There was a slight pause before they all burst out laughing.

Back at the gite, Cameron dried off and then turned the TV on.

"It'll be all in French," Coral remarked.

"I should try and see if I can understand it. Otherwise, what's the point of learning French at school?" Cameron responded.

49

So they sat for a while, but everyone seemed to be speaking too quickly. Cameron picked up a few words, but in the end, he gave up.

"I think that they speak a different sort of French to the French that I've been learning," he sighed. "I can't understand any of it." So the TV was turned off and never switched on again.

However, he was able to help out a little bit later when the owner of the gite called to make sure that they were happy with everything. "Cameron, can you help us here?" Mrs Browne called.

When he appeared at the door, the lady started speaking again. "Lentement, s'il vous plait," Cameron said. She repeated it slowly, and then Cameron was able to work out what she was saying. He translated both ways, French to English, English to French. Mrs Browne and Madame shook hands. Madame looked at Cameron, smiled and said, "Bonne." Then to them all, "Au revoir."

Coral was smiling, "I bet you're glad we brought him now, mum."

Chapter: 7

The next day dawned sunny, and after breakfast, they decided to walk to Arromanches along the beach. Holding hands, Coral and Cameron dawdled behind her parents. Mrs Browne smiled to herself as she heard them laughing, and on one occasion, as she turned around, she caught them standing still and having a kiss. Coral noticed.

She laughed, "Mum! Stop watching."

It took them just over half an hour to reach the little town. As they got closer, the remains of the wartime Mulberry Harbour became much clearer. Time, weather and the sea had taken their toll on what was left, and with large holes in the side, it was obvious that none of the concrete blocks would ever float again as they had once done. Cameron could see what looked like the remains of a machine gun on one of them. As the tide was out, they could get quite close to a couple of them. Mr Browne explained that they had been built in secret, and after D Day towed across the channel to form a temporary harbour so that troops, tanks and goods could be brought ashore. Cameron was fascinated.

Then they went to explore the town, which was packed with tourists, mostly English. It seemed as if everywhere they went, they could hear English being spoken, but sometimes with an American accent. The gift shops were full of souvenirs that celebrated D Day. Cameron wanted to buy something for his dad as he knew that he would be interested in the story of D Day. He took a photograph of the front window of one shop that had a banner across the top proclaiming 'Welcome to our British Liberators'

They found a nice little bistro where they decided to have lunch. Mr Browne passed the menu to Cameron. "What's on the menu, Cameron?"

Cameron studied it for a few seconds, then read out, "Ham baguettes, salad baguettes, tuna baguettes, fish and chips, ham egg and chips and lots of other things as well."

As Cameron passed the menu back to him, Mr Browne said, "Good job, you're here. It didn't take you long to translate that." Cameron was almost laughing now, and Mr Browne looked at him and then again at the menu.

He started to smile. "Ah...I see. There is an English translation under each item. No wonder you were so quick."

"And I thought that you were being clever, Cameron," laughed Mrs Browne.

Coral kissed him on the cheek, "He is clever," she smiled.

After lunch, Mr Browne said, "Have you had enough history? Only there is a museum here that tells you the whole story of D Day."

Before Coral or Cameron could answer, Mrs Browne spoke up. "It's a lovely day. It could rain later in the week, and then we might need to find something to do indoors. The museum would be good then. Let's explore here for a little while and then go back along the cliffs." "Good idea, mum." So that's what they did.

When eventually they thought they had seen all there was to see of Arromanches, they took the path out of the town that led up to the cliffs. At the top of the path, they found an American tank. Cameron made Coral stand by it whilst he took her photograph.

Also on the clifftop was the Circular Cinema. After reading all the information (in English) about the cinema, Mr Browne said, "Another place for a rainy day."

They were in no rush to get back to the gite. The views from the cliffs were beautiful. They stopped several times as there were plenty of benches to sit on.

The following morning looked promising weather-wise, so Mrs Browne suggested that perhaps they should go and find the cemetery at Ranville. After breakfast, they set off and more or less drove back the way they had come from the port. It didn't take too long to reach Pegasus Bridge.

"This bridge is where the first battle of D Day was fought and where my uncle was killed," announced Mr Browne, "That building over there, the café, was the first building in France to be liberated. Café Gondree. We'll stop there on the way back."

The cemetery was immaculately kept. Not a blade of grass was out of place. There was row after row of white headstones, each with a tiny flower bed in front of it. Each headstone had a soldier's name on it and the regiment in which he served.

"There are so many. How will we find the one we are looking for?" asked Mrs Browne.

"We'll just have to split up and take rows each," Mr Browne replied.

In the event, it didn't take too long, and it was Coral who found him. It didn't seem right to shout, so she waved, trying to attract their attention. It was Mrs Browne who spotted her first, and she managed to catch the attention of the other two. They went and joined Coral, who stood in front of the last resting place of

Bernard G Freeman

Royal Corps of Signals

June 6th 1944

aged 24.

Mr Browne placed a small wooden cross and a silk poppy in the flower bed in front of the headstone. "He was my mother's brother," he said quietly. After a while, they moved away, and Cameron took them to another headstone that had particularly caught his attention. "Look at this one." They read the inscription:

R E John

Parachute Regiment

June 6th 1944

aged 16.

Cameron almost whispered, "I didn't know that you could join up so young."

"Officially, you couldn't, but some boys lied about their ages just so they could join. When they were found out, it was often too late to do anything about it," Mr Browne replied.

"I'll soon be 16," Cameron said quietly.

They spent a little more time just wandering. It was so peaceful, and although a sad place, it did not feel morbid.

Cameron was in awe of the bravery of these men who fought so long ago.

Coral was by his side as they were leaving. "I'm glad there are no wars now. I wouldn't want you to have to join the army."

"I could choose to join, though," he said, smiling at her.

"No, I don't want you to."

"The navy then?"

"No, you would be away for ages and ages."

"What about the air force then?"

"No, not that either and stop teasing me." He waited till they were actually in the car park before he kissed her and said, "Okay, I won't join any of the forces then."

"GOOD," was all she said.

They did stop at Café Gondree for lunch. The café itself was almost like a museum with black and white photographs hanging on the wall. There was also some wartime memorabilia displayed in cases on little tables. Cameron was fascinated by the story of this little café and how it was still owned by the same family after all these years.

On the way back to the gite, they stopped several times at a couple of the little seaside villages with their nice sandy beaches, interesting little harbours and a few souvenir shops to browse.

By the time they got back, it was time for something to eat. Afterwards, they sat for a while. Mrs Browne noticed that Cameron was rather quiet.

"Are you alright, Cameron?" she enquired. "You are very quiet."

"I'm fine, thank you. I was just thinking about this morning. You see war films on TV, and you know that when the filming stops, all the actors get up and walk away. In the cemetery this morning, you realise that all those men did not get up and walk away. There must have been thousands more like them. It makes you think."

"It certainly does," Mr Browne responded.

As far as he was concerned, Mr Browne felt he had done the most important part of the holiday, so now he was quite happy to spend the rest of the time doing whatever his wife and the youngsters wanted.

Mrs Browne said that she wanted to visit Bayeux to see the tapestry, so they spent a day in Bayeux. Mrs Browne and Coral were amazed by the tapestry. Mrs Browne remarked that she had never realised that it was almost seventy metres long. Cameron bought a tapestry kit for his mum. He chose the section where Harold got the arrow in his eye. Coral said that was horrible. Cameron said it was history. He also bought a similar one for Mrs Browne to give to her when they got back home. Later after lunch, they visited the cathedral and then explored the pretty little back streets where most of the houses were decorated with window boxes in full bloom.

For the rest of the holiday, they visited some of the attractive little coastal villages, walked along cliff tops and because Cameron had picked up several folded advertising leaflets about WW2 sites, they visited a few of them too. St Mere Eglise was interesting because an American paratrooper had got his parachute caught on the church steeple and had to play dead whilst watching the battle below and hope that the Americans won it, which they did, and he was rescued. "He was one lucky soldier," Mr Browne remarked.

A dummy paratrooper and parachute are permanently placed on the church steeple as a reminder.

The beautiful American cemetery at Omaha Beach was quite nearby, and so they visited that and were surprised by the size of it. Almost 10,000 Americans were buried there. They were very quiet as they wandered around the paths between the thousands of pure white crosses and the immaculately kept grass.

Soon, too soon for Cameron and Coral, the holiday was over, and they were packing to leave. Cameron gave Mrs Browne the tapestry kit that he had bought for her rather than waiting until they were back home. She hugged him.

"You shouldn't have Cameron," but secretly, she was delighted. He gave Mr Browne a small bottle of Normandie Cidre.

"I hope you like it, Mr Browne."

"Thank you, Cameron. I WON'T say, 'You shouldn't have'," he replied with a smile. The next day they were on the 4.30 pm ferry out of Caen. As they watched the French coastline disappear into the distance, Mrs Browne asked, "Well, you two, have you had a good time?" They both nodded.

"It's been lovely, mum. The best holiday I've ever had."

"I wonder why?" pondered Mr Browne trying to keep a smile off his face. He adored his daughter, and he knew that he had never seen her so happy. Even he had begun to think that this romance might last. Secretly, he had to admit to himself that he was beginning to think that it might and that he would be disappointed if it didn't.

Chapter: 8

They arrived home in the early hours of the morning. Cameron thanked the Brownes again for a lovely time, kissed Coral good morning and walked down the street to number 27. He didn't need to knock. His mum had worked out roughly what time they would be back, and she had got up early to welcome him home. She had seen the car pull up and opened the door as he walked up the drive.

"Have you had a good time?"

"Yes, mum, it's been great, and before you ask, I've behaved myself. I'll tell you all about it later, but can I go and get some sleep now?"

When he got up, he had something to eat. He gave his mum the tapestry kit and his dad the souvenir book about the D Day landings. Then they got a full report of the whole holiday. It was early evening before Coral turned up at the front door. Mrs Mason opened it. "Hello, Coral. Did you have a good holiday?"

"Yes, thank you, Mrs Mason. It was the best ever." Mrs Mason smiled. "Come in, love. We've already heard about it from Cameron, but I'm sure you'll want to tell us all about it."

She did tell them all about it. Later, when Mr and Mrs Mason were alone, she said, "Did you notice how much the two of them laughed when she was telling the tale, and the looks they kept giving each other?"

"I did, and I also noticed how Cameron looks at her when she's not looking. He absolutely adores her."

"I think that I already knew that," Mrs Mason replied.

A few days later, Cameron was knocking at the Brownes' door. Coral opened it and kissed him.

"Come in. Mum, it's Cameron." Her dad's voice came from somewhere. "Who else would it be?"

Cameron looked at Coral.

"Dad," she said laughing, "Don't be so rude." Mrs Browne appeared, "Come in love, take no notice of him." When they entered the room, her dad looked up from his paper.

He was smiling, "Hello Cameron, it seems ages since I last saw you."

"DAD, stop it!"

"Have you recovered from the journey, Cameron?" Cameron nodded, "Yes, thank you, Mr Browne. I've brought the photos for you to look at. I've had two sets developed,

61

one set for you and one set for me," and he handed a pack of photos to Mrs Browne. "You can have this set."

They spent a good few minutes laughing and reminiscing about the holiday as they passed the photos around.

"There seem to be rather a lot of Coral, or a lot of Cameron and not too many of the other two members of the party," Mr Browne remarked with a smile.

"I don't mind that," Mrs Browne replied. "They must have had a good time. Look at all the smiles."

Later Cameron said, "Tomorrow we are going to visit my dad's cousin, Uncle Ben. He lives by the seaside. He's a bit eccentric, but I like him. Mum wondered if Coral would like to come with us."

Before she could answer, her dad butted in.

"That's a daft question, Cameron. Spend a day at the seaside with you, or have a boring day at home with us?"

Coral looked at her mum. "It's up to you love."

"Yes, please."

"Told you," laughed her dad.

Cameron explained about Uncle Ben. "He's very clever. He's an engineer. He had his own engineering company, which he sold for an awful lot of money. Dad won't tell me how much. He's supposed to be retired now, but he still comes up with great ideas and then sells them, usually to the aerospace companies, and then makes even more money. His house is massive. I don't know why he needs such a big house, because he lives by himself. Dad is his only relative. Dad says he's a ladies man, so if Coral comes, she'd better watch out. The best bit of his house is one of the rooms upstairs. It's got a great model railway in it."

"He sounds an interesting gentleman," Mr Browne remarked. "Watch out for yourself," he said, looking at Coral.

Cameron was right. The house was big. There were no houses like it near where they lived, Coral thought. It even had two gateways so that you could drive in and out without having to turn the car around. There were flower beds all along the edge of the drive, and they were filled with a variety of summer flowers. Coral thought that it looked lovely. There was a wide stone flight of steps up to the front door. Cameron rang the bell, and a few seconds later, the big heavy wooden door opened, and there was Uncle Ben.

Cameron was right again, thought Coral. He was very tall, had bright blue eyes, a bushy moustache. He was wearing a blue check shirt and cravat, Rupert trousers and big heavy brown shoes. Coral also noticed that he wore several rings and an expensive-looking gold watch. His face lit up with a big smile when he saw them.

"Good to see you all," he said in a deep voice. He turned to Coral, "and who is this delightful young lady?"

Cameron answered, "This is Coral, Uncle Ben." Uncle Ben took hold of Coral's hand and kissed her fingers.

"Very nice to meet you, Coral. Come in, all of you. Close the door behind you, Cameron," and still holding Coral's hand, he led them into the house.

"We'll use this room, I think. Sit yourselves down whilst Coral and I go and make a brew, and she can tell me all about herself," and he led her off into the kitchen. Left behind, the three of them sat down. Mr Mason shook his head in despair.

"All it takes is a pretty face, and he puts on his act," he said smiling.

Meanwhile, in the kitchen, all they could hear was Coral laughing. "He's a bit of a rogue, your uncle," chuckled Mrs Mason. Shortly afterwards, they reappeared, Coral with a tray of biscuits and Uncle Ben with the teapot and cups on a larger tray. Mrs Mason offered to pour, and while they were enjoying the tea, Uncle Ben insisted that Coral and Cameron tell him all about the holiday in France.

When they had finished, he said, "I've just got to make a phone call. We are going out for lunch. I didn't realise that there would be five of us. I only booked for four, so I'll just phone ahead and let them know. BUT, by the way, I am delighted that there are five of us. It's always nice to have a pretty face around."

They walked to the restaurant. Coral had never been anywhere like it. It looked expensive. Uncle Ben was obviously well known to the staff as they hovered around him attentively and ushered the five of them to a table with a window view. Uncle Ben insisted that Coral sat next to him, so Cameron made sure that he sat on the other side of Coral.

"You can order whatever you like," Uncle Ben announced to them all but seemed to direct it mainly at Coral. There was so much to choose from and some of the items on the menu she had never even heard of. She chose something that she knew she would like.

"Seafood pie, please."

"A good choice," remarked Uncle Ben. "I'll have the same."

As the meal progressed, Cameron realised that by asking harmless questions, his uncle was learning all about Coral.

By the end of the meal, he probably knew everything there was to know about her.

When they were ready to leave the restaurant, Uncle Ben turned to Cameron's mum and said, "Louise, you take these two off for a couple of hours, whilst Steve and I go back to the house. I've got something that I want to show and discuss with him. You'd all find it boring. If you're back before we've finished, you can always go and play trains," he said, smiling at Cameron. "I've added to it since you last saw it, Cameron."

Uncle Ben and Mr Mason headed back to the house, but the other three wandered to the seafront. They found an 18 hole putting green course, so they had a game. Cameron realised that Coral was very competitive and was desperate to win the game. They gasped and moaned at near misses, but the best thing was that all three of them laughed a lot. In the end, Mrs Mason was the winner. They walked along the promenade, watched children having fun on the bouncy castles, and families on the lake in self-drive motorboats. Cameron persuaded Coral that she wanted a ride on the miniature railway, and then they called in at the café for a drink.

Back at the house, His dad and uncle had not quite finished, so Cameron took Coral to see the model railway. It was much larger than she had expected as it almost filled the room. There was just enough space around the edge of the room to be able to reach any derailments. It wasn't just a railway track. It was landscaped with buildings, lakes, fields, animals and people, all to scale. Cameron showed Coral how it all worked, and she gingerly had a go with the controller. She was quite pleased that she managed to get the train completely around the track without a mishap.

Back downstairs, the little meeting was over, and they were all back together in the same room as before when there was a ring of the doorbell. Uncle Ben answered it and returned, followed by two ladies carrying trays of food.

"Afternoon tea," he announced.

"Coral, would you like to help me brew up." She nodded and followed him into the kitchen. The food was lovely, and then it was time to leave. On the steps, he wished them a safe journey and kissed Coral on the back of her hand again.

"I hope to see you again, Coral," he smiled.

As Cameron was going down the steps, Uncle Ben called him back. He pushed a bundle of notes into his hand and said, "You've got a diamond there. Don't you dare go and lose her. You won't find another girl like Coral and use this to treat her."

"Thanks, Uncle Ben. I know she's lovely and I will treat her. Thank you."

In the car, his dad asked, "What was all that about?"

"Nothing really," Cameron replied. Once on the way, Mr Mason asked, "Well Coral, did you enjoy the day?"

"Yes, thank you. Your uncle is funny. He makes me laugh, and he's generous. In the kitchen, he gave me £40 and told me to treat Cameron. I said I couldn't take it because it was too much. He said if I didn't take it, he would push it down the front of my blouse, so I took it!" They all laughed.

"He's a right rogue Ben," smiled Mr Mason.

When Cameron got home, he looked at his bundle of notes for the first time. There was £40.

In the evening, when the Masons were together, Cameron asked his dad what he and Uncle Ben talked about during the afternoon.

"He's got another idea in his head, and if it works, and I think it will, he will make a lot more money when he sells it to the aircraft industry."

Meanwhile, Coral was telling her parents all about her day out. "Cameron's uncle is a lovely man. He's a bit odd and funny, but he's very generous. I think he must be quite rich. Cameron said he lived in a big house, but it was even bigger than I expected. When he opened the door to let us in, I thought that his clothes were a bit colourful. He has a big moustache. When Cameron introduced me, he kissed me on the hand. No one has ever done that to me before, not even Cameron. He took us out for a lovely lunch at an expensive restaurant, and later before we came home, he had afternoon tea delivered. He got me to help in the kitchen. He told me to make sure that I didn't lose Cameron, and he gave me this to treat him." She showed them the £40.

Her mum gasped, "Coral, you shouldn't have taken it. That's a lot of money."

"I tried not to, but he said that if I didn't take it, he would push it down my blouse. So I thought that I'd better take it. I did say thank you." There was a look of horror on her mum's face, but her dad was smiling.

"He sounds like a bit of a character, this Uncle Ben."

One afternoon, when they were walking in the country park that could be reached from the canal towpath, Cameron asked her, "If you had lots of money, what would you buy for yourself?"

She thought for a while, then said, "I would really like a collie dog, but mum and dad say that a pet is too tying. Why do you ask?"

"No reason, really. So if you can't have a pet, what then." By now, she was beginning to work it out.

"Your uncle gave you some money and said you had to treat me. That's right, isn't it?" He nodded. There was a pause, and then she said, "Let's save it and buy something between us." So that was what they agreed to do.

Chapter: 9

After the summer, things got back to normal - school, obviously. 'The Gang' meetings resumed at the Browne's or at another house, and the youth club restarted. Everybody seemed to have had a good summer, and there was a lot to talk about and catch up with. The boys, in particular, were interested in the war stuff and looked at the photos that Cameron had carefully selected from the pack. There weren't too many of him and Coral in the selection. However, he made sure that there were a few of the two cemeteries they had visited. Like Cameron, they were surprised at the size of them, especially the American one. "There were lots of smaller British ones dotted all over," he told them.

With Remembrance Sunday approaching, he made sure that he bought a poppy. When Coral saw it, she said, "I'll get one from school next week." When the day arrived, Cameron persuaded his parents to take him into town to watch the service at the War Memorial. Of course, Coral went with them. It was all very impressive, with the military band leading the veterans to the memorial garden. Then there was the silence signalled by the bugler, followed by the laying of the wreaths and the march past.

"After what we saw in France, I'm glad that we went this morning," he said on the way home. Coral was quiet but nodded.

A few weeks later, the bottom fell out of Cameron's world when he came home from school one day, and his parents made him sit down. "Cameron, we've got something to tell you," his mum said. He looked at them. "Your dad has got a new job," she went on.

"That's great, Dad. Well done, you." They both looked at him.

"What!" he said.

It was his mum who spoke. "We're going to have to move, Cameron, love. The job is at the other factory, down near Bristol."

There was a stunned silence, and then Cameron dashed out of the room, ran upstairs, and threw himself face down on his bed. *This must be the worst day of my life,* he thought. *No friends and miles away from Coral.* His mind was in a whirl. How was he going to tell Coral? He tried to think of scenarios that could keep him up here whilst his mum and dad were down there. His common sense told him that none of them would have the slightest chance of working.

After a few minutes, there was a knock on his door, and his mum came in and sat on the edge of the bed.

"Cameron, it's a great opportunity for your dad, and it's a lot more money. He can't turn it down." He turned to face her, and she could see that his eyes were red.

"I get that, Mum, and I'm pleased for dad, but...." his voice trailed off.

"It's Coral you're thinking about, isn't it?"

He nodded.

"We knew that would be a big problem, and we understand that. She's a lovely girl, and we will miss her almost as much as you will. I went to see Mrs Browne this morning and told her about us having to move. She was a bit shocked, and she knew that Coral would be very upset, so we've agreed that every school holiday you can get together. Either Coral can come to us, or you can come back here. It's the best we can do." Cameron nodded. "Mrs Browne said that it would be better for you to tell Coral what's happening."

He shook his head. "Mum, how am I going to tell her? What am I going to say?" There was a pause. She shook her head.

"I don't know, Cameron, but you'll have to tell her soon. We are putting the house up for sale this week, so she needs to know before she sees the sign."

"When is all this going to happen?" he asked.

"More or less straight after Christmas," she answered.

***

Coral and Cameron went for a walk along the towpath. He was holding her hand as if he would never let go. They reached one of their favourite spots under the canal bridge. He turned to face her, put his arms around her, kissed her, and then asked, "Coral, you do love me, don't you?" She gave him a strange look.

"Of course, I do, silly. You know that. Why are you asking?"

"Coral, I don't really know how to tell you this. It's bad news…the worst news ever. Dad has got a new job, and we are going to have to move."

She looked at him. He could see fear in her eyes.

"Where to?" she whispered.

"Near Bristol." She threw her arms around him and burst out crying. They walked home in silence. When they got back to her house, he pulled her to him and said, "Coral, whatever happens, I promise that I will come back for you," and he kissed her.

"Promise?" she said.

"I promise" was his answer, and he meant it.

***

Coral's mum had been expecting her, and when she heard the gate shut, she dashed into the hall. She was waiting for Coral as she opened the front door. Mrs Browne could see that she had been crying, and she held her tight. Coral looked up at her mum.

"You knew," she said accusingly, "you knew that's why you're here waiting for me."

"Yes, I knew. Mrs Mason came to tell me this morning, but I thought that it was better if Cameron told you."

"Mum, what am I going to do? I really love Cameron, and he's going to be miles away. I might never see him again after they've moved."

"You will see him again, love. His mum and I have already sorted it. You can visit each other in the school holidays. He can come here, or you can go there. Your dad and I like Cameron. You know that. As long as you two want to be together, we will do our best to help. We know it will be hard, but if you do love each other, everything will work out in the end."

By this time, her dad had appeared. "Come here, Coral," and he held out his arms and hugged her.

"Cameron has promised to come back for me," she whispered.

He looked down at her.

"If that's what he's said, then I believe him," her dad said. "I believe him," he said again.

Chapter: 10

The news spread quickly. There was disappointment all around. The girls were worried. How will Coral manage without Cameron? The boys pointed out that Coral would still have the rest of them for friends, and it was Cameron who they should be thinking about. Not only would he miss Coral, but he would have to make new friends as well. They thought that it was going to be much harder for Cameron.

When it was put like that, the girls agreed with the boys. They decided that they would arrange a party for them. The question was, where and when? The youth club would obviously be holding its own Christmas party, and they knew that the Masons were moving in the New Year, so fitting it in might be a problem. Another problem was who to invite. Tony suggested that it should be just the eight of them, and the others agreed, but where should they hold it? A few days later, they had the answer; Gordon's mum said that they could have it there the day before New Year's Eve.

For Cameron and Coral, the time seemed to fly by. They spent every spare minute that they had together. They talked about plans. Coral knew that she was going to try and go to Edinburgh University to be a vet. "It's supposed to be one of the best," she told him, "but it takes five years to qualify." Cameron wasn't sure which university he wanted to go to or what to study. He knew it would be science and probably chemistry. However, he was worried. Edinburgh seemed an awfully long way away. How would they stay in touch?

"Let's not worry about that now. That's a long time off yet," she said. "While we are still at school, our mums have said that we can visit each other during the holidays. We'll just have to make do with that." She looked at him. "Cameron, I love you. We'll manage somehow…kiss me."

***

The day before the Masons were due to leave, the furniture van arrived, and Coral watched for a while as all of the Masons' belongings were being loaded up. Then she couldn't bear it any longer and retreated to her room. The Masons were left with just three sleeping bags, blow-up air beds, a change of clothes, toiletries, and enough food for breakfast the next morning. In the evening, there was no alternative for them but to eat out. Coral was invited, but it was a very subdued occasion. When they got back home, Cameron walked her to the door. He reached inside his jacket pocket and pulled out a small parcel.

"This is for you," he said as he handed it over. She opened it. Inside was a locket and chain. She opened the locket, and inside there were two pictures; one of him and another of her that were taken in France. She looked at him with tears in her eyes.

"Cameron, thank you. I'm going to miss you so much. I'll wear this always. I promise."

He kissed her. "I know that I've said it before, but I will come back for you, Coral, no matter what happens." And he kissed her again. They held on to each other for ages, and then Coral kissed him, turned and fled indoors. Inside, Mr and Mrs Browne heard her dash upstairs. They looked at each other.

"Best leave her awhile," her dad said, but it wasn't too long before Mrs Browne went up to comfort her.

The dreaded day had arrived. After breakfast, all that was left to do was pack up the car and leave. When it was obvious that the departure was imminent, Mr and Mrs Browne and Coral walked down to the Masons to say their goodbyes. There were a few tears from both mums, as, after all, they had been friends and neighbours a long time. The men shook hands and wished each other good luck.

Mrs Browne gave Cameron a big hug and whispered in his ear, "She'll wait for you, you know." He nodded.

Mrs Mason hugged Coral. "We'll see you soon, love. Things will work out, I'm sure."

Coral grabbed Cameron's hand and pulled him to her. She kissed him and whispered in his ear, "I love you, Cameron."

"I love you too," he replied, and he gave her another parcel. "Don't open it now; wait till we've gone. What is in it will look after you for me." He kissed her again, and then it was time to leave.

The Brownes waved them off, and then Coral dashed inside to open her present. It was a beautiful little teddy bear about the size that you would give to a baby. She showed it to her mum and then hugged it to herself. Then she took it upstairs and placed it on her pillow, lay down on the bed and cried.

Mr and Mrs Browne were well aware that Coral would find the next few weeks very difficult. Over the last two years or so, Cameron and Coral had seen each other virtually every day. They were amazed at how well they had got on. As far as they knew, they had never once had an argument. They knew that she would need a lot of support. Coral also knew that it was going to be hard without Cameron. *I'm a bit luckier than Cameron*, she thought; *I've still got my friends while Cameron will have to try and make new ones.* She decided that she needed more than her schoolwork and the youth club to fill her time. But what?

She thought about it for a while and then made a decision. She wrote to the three vet surgeries in the area, explaining that she wanted to be a vet and wondered if there was anything she could do on a voluntary basis to help out. If there was, it would be something that she could add to her application when the time came to fill in the forms for university.

Coral told her parents what she had done. They were pleased but warned her not to be too disappointed if nothing came of it. A few days later, she got a reply. To her disappointment, it was a polite refusal, but it did wish her success in the future. Then nothing else for several days, and Coral began to feel a little downhearted.

Chapter: 11

Early one evening, the phone rang, and her dad answered it. Coral was up in her room when her dad called her down. He had a smile on his face.

"It's for you," he told her. She was sure it would be Cameron.

"Is it Cameron?" she asked. He shook his head. Puzzled, she took the phone off him.

"Hello."

There was a female voice at the other end.

"Hello, Coral. My name is Hannah Chadwick, and I am one of the vets at the Fiveways Surgery. It's about your letter. We are very impressed with your initiative, Coral, and we would like to talk to you. We cannot promise you anything, but would you like to come to the surgery so that we can meet you?"

Coral didn't hesitate. "Yes, please."

"Very well then; the surgery closes at 1 o'clock on Saturday. Can you be here at 1.15 p.m. next Saturday?"

"Yes, thank you. I'll be there."

"Good. The door will be locked; just ring the bell. I'll look forward to seeing you, Coral. Goodnight."

Coral put the phone down and turned around. Her mum was there. "Well," she asked.

"They want to talk to me; I've got to be at the surgery at 1.15 p.m. on Saturday," she said with a smile, "but they're not promising anything."

Her mum hugged her. "I'm sure that they will once they've met you."

Saturday couldn't come soon enough for Coral, and then Saturday morning seemed to drag. Normally, she would have gone and watched the boys play football, but now that Cameron wasn't in the team, it didn't seem to have the same attraction. She lay on her bed or mooched around the house. She just couldn't settle.

Eventually, her mum said, "For goodness's sake, Coral, do something useful and hoover the front room." So she did.

She was so nervous that she didn't eat much at lunchtime and then got herself ready. She wasn't sure what to wear. She didn't want to look like a schoolgirl, but she didn't want to look as though she was too grown-up or look as if she was going to a party. Eventually, she settled on a pair of dark trousers and a slightly pink blouse with a faint floral pattern. She asked her mum what she thought. "You look just right. Do you want me to come with you?"

"No, Mum, I want them to think that I am grown up and don't need anyone to support me."

Her dad nodded. "She's right, you know. She'll be alright on her own."

At exactly 1.15 p.m., she rang the bell of the surgery, and a few seconds later, the door opened. Coral was slightly surprised. In front of her, there was someone much younger than she expected. Coral guessed that she might be in her late twenties or early thirties. She gave Coral a welcoming smile.

"Come in; you must be Coral. I'm Hannah," and they shook hands. "Come through to the backroom; we use it as a bit of a staff room. Now sit down and tell me all about yourself."

Coral told her about always wanting to be a vet and how she had learned from the careers teacher at school that it took five years, and Edinburgh was one of the best places to go. When asked about what else she did, she told Hannah about the youth club and how they came to do first aid and self-defence.

Suddenly she stopped. "I'm talking too much, aren't I?"

Hannah laughed, "No, Coral, you are an interesting young lady. We've never had a request like this before, but I liked your letter. Did you write to anywhere else?"

Coral nodded. "One replied and said no; you rang me, and I haven't heard from the others."

"Now, I have to be honest. I have done a little bit of research on you." Coral looked puzzled. Hannah continued, "Does my surname ring a bell with you?" Coral was about to say no when she remembered.

"One of my teachers at school is Miss Chadwick."

"That's right; she's my sister, and I asked her if she knew you. You will be pleased to know that she thinks very highly of you."

Coral was a bit embarrassed. "I do try to work hard," she said.

"I believe you, Coral, so I am going to offer you a kind of work experience at the surgery. How does that sound?" Coral was smiling, "It sounds good, thank you."

So, it was agreed. Coral would attend the surgery every Saturday morning for two months in the first place, and then it would be reviewed. Hannah told her how the surgery worked. There were three vets in practice, but Hannah was the only one who worked on a Saturday morning. Coral had to be there at 8:30 a.m. and stay until the last patient was seen. There was a receptionist who looked after the office and the waiting room. Hannah said she would introduce them the following week. There was one more thing; when they were alone, Coral could call her Hannah, but when the pets' owners were around, she should call her Miss Chadwick. Finally, she said, "Is there anything else that you want to know?"

"What should I wear?" Coral asked.

"Something similar to what you have on now will do, and we will lend you an overall. Now that's enough for now, I think." There was a pause.

"Coral, I have a good feeling about this, so I'll see you next week."

Coral almost skipped home. She was pleased with herself and couldn't wait to tell her mum and dad and later on, on the phone to Cameron, she went through the whole meeting almost word for word. Cameron could tell that she was excited, and he said, "What did you expect? You're clever, Coral. Once she'd met you, she'd know that you were serious. She sounds nice, though. I'm really pleased for you."

Chapter: 12

In school the following week, Miss Chadwick kept Coral back at the end of a lesson. "My sister tells me that she's offered you some sort of work experience, Coral."

"Yes, miss, I am going to start Saturday morning."

"I hope that you enjoy it and it doesn't put you off from being a vet. It takes a lot of hard work, you know."

Coral nodded. "I know that, miss, and thank you for saying nice things about me to your sister."

"That's fine, Coral, and believe me, it wasn't difficult," she said with a smile.

***

There was a new family living in Mason's old house. Coral found it difficult to walk past without thinking of Cameron. As far as she could make out, it was a family of three, and the boy looked about the same age as Cameron. She had seen him a few times, often riding up and down the street on his bike.

After school one afternoon, she was returning home with a bit of shopping that her mum had sent her for. The boy was in the front garden with his bike upside down.

"Having a bit of a problem?" she asked him. He seemed a bit startled, as though he hadn't realised that she was there.

"I've got a puncture," he replied.

She laughed. "That's a shame, but I can't help you with that."

She was about to move on when he said, "I'm Luke."

"And I'm Coral," she replied.

"It's nice to meet you, Coral, and I mean that." She looked at him.

"Oh, why's that?" she asked.

"I didn't want to move here. I've had to leave all my friends behind. I think that you are about the only person that's spoken to me so far apart from some at school."

"Cameron is having the same trouble," she said.

"Who's Cameron?"

"He is my boyfriend. He used to live in your house, but they've moved miles away. He's finding it hard to make new friends." She took pity on him.

"There's a youth club that meets on a Saturday evening. Why don't you come? I'll introduce you to everyone. It starts at 6 o'clock...no, it doesn't! It starts at 7 o'clock; the self-defence starts at six, but nearly everyone goes to the class. I'll explain why if you're interested."

He was interested, so the following Saturday, Luke went with Coral to the youth club. She introduced him to her friends.

"This is Luke. He's living in Cameron's house."

Luckily, Luke fitted in well and was soon regarded as one of the gang - so much so that he was included in the Friday meetings at the Browne's or wherever they were being held. Mrs Browne had decided that even though Cameron was no longer around, it would be wrong to stop the meetings. Jenny, in particular, seemed pleased that Luke was around and had confided in Coral more than once that he was 'cute'.

Luke, however, tried to raise the level of his friendship with Coral and tried asking her out on several occasions, but Coral was having none of it. "We can be friends," she told him, "but nothing more."

Ian had noticed that Luke was trying hard to get closer to Coral and told him that he was wasting his time.

"Coral loves Cameron and Cameron loves Coral. I can't see that changing ever. One day they will get married, believe me."

Eventually, Coral said to Luke, "It doesn't matter how often you ask me, I won't go out with you; that is just us on our own. Cameron is my boyfriend. Why don't you ask Jenny out? She's liked you almost since the first night at the club."

Luke finally realised that he would just have to accept the friendship with Coral on her terms and gave up trying to pressurise her. A little while later, he did ask Jenny out.

***

Coral was really enjoying her Saturday mornings at the surgery. Hannah was secretly pleased to see that when Coral arrived the first morning, she had a notebook with her. Hannah explained the rules that Coral would have to work to. Obviously, she could not handle drugs or be involved in any surgical procedures, but she could watch and listen to consultations. Hannah was pleased to see that after she had examined or treated some, not all of the animals, Coral often made notes. Most of the patients were small domestic pets, such as hamsters, gerbils or rabbits, but sometimes, a dog or a cat arrived. Coral took it upon herself to tidy the waiting room at the end of the morning, allowing Sophie, the receptionist, to finish the paperwork for the day. At the end of each shift, she always asked if there was anything else that she could do before she went home. One lunchtime, before she left, Hannah gave Coral a parcel.

"Here," she said, "you might find this interesting. It's a book and is considered to be the vets' bible. You can borrow it. When you get to university, you will almost certainly need your own copy."

At home, Coral opened the parcel. The book was called 'Textbook of Veterinary Anatomy' by KM Dyce. There were over 800 pages in it with drawings and photographs as well as the text.

***

Chapter: 13

Cameron knew that he would miss Coral terribly. What he hadn't realised was how much he would miss the rest of his friends. For the first time in his life, he wasn't happy at school. In the past, he had been popular, and it wasn't that he deliberately set out to be popular. It was something that happened naturally. People just seemed to like his company. He was able to get on with most people, perhaps because he had known them all for ages.

Here in his new school, he found it difficult to make friends. He knew no one. It wasn't that the other students were unfriendly; it was just the fact that most of them had been together for years, and just like 'The Gang' back home, the friendship groups here were rock-solid, and he understood that. However, understanding the problem didn't help solve it.

At home, his parents realised that as far as Cameron was concerned, the move hadn't gone well. They noticed that he was much quieter, and he often retreated to his room, where he would read for hours on end. He had always enjoyed reading, but now he read far more than he had ever done before. His parents both knew that he was missing Coral, and his dad tried to gloss over it.

"He'll find another girl before long, just you see," he told his wife.

"I don't think he will," she replied. Secretly, Mr Mason wasn't so sure himself.

She went on. "It's not just Coral, though. He doesn't seem to be making friends. He never goes out, never talks about anyone in his classes. It's as though he has become a loner and our Cameron was never a loner."

"Well, we'll just have to encourage him to join things. There must be football clubs around that he could get involved with. He is a good player after all," his dad responded.

Cameron and Coral had promised to write to each other, and they did. Cameron was noticeably brighter after he received letters from Coral, although the effect soon wore off. There was also the occasional phone call between them that often lasted a long time, but it was not the same as being together.

Cameron did try hard not to let all this affect his schoolwork, although he wasn't doing quite as well as he had done back home. Wednesday afternoon turned out to be his favourite time - games lessons and a chance to get out and play football. That was something else that he missed as well; football on a Saturday morning.

The first Wednesday afternoon after he started at the school, since he was new, the PE teacher put him in the group with the boys who weren't really that bothered about football. However, the teacher in charge of that particular group soon realised that he had talent, and he gradually got promoted through the groups. By week four, he was playing with those who really wanted to play.

Half term was approaching, and at lunchtime on the Monday before the Friday finish, Cameron suddenly found Edwards facing him across the table. Edwards was a big lad, a VERY big lad. Cameron had seen him around and heard the others talking about him. He had two other lads with him who were equally as big and stood on either side of him. Cameron didn't know either of them.

"You're new, aren't you, Mason?" Cameron nodded. "Well, this is how it works. On Friday, you will pay me £2."

Cameron looked at him. "Oh! And why would I do that?"

"It's protection money. You pay me, and we'll protect you."

"I can look after myself, thanks. So, I'll not pay you anything, and anyway, who am I being protected from?"

Edwards leaned towards Cameron, made a fist, and holding it near Cameron's face, he said, "From ME, so £2 at the gate on Friday after school, or you'll regret it."

"No chance," Cameron replied.

During the week, Cameron discovered that this protection racket had been going on for ages, and no one had dared to stand up to them or dared to report it.

"Well, I'm not paying him," he said to the little group who had passed on the information, "and I'm not scared of him either."

Word got around that Cameron was not going to 'cough' up the protection money, and as Friday grew closer, Cameron could feel that there was tension in the air. Gary, one of the boys from the football group, came and sat by him at lunchtime.

"I'd pay up if I was you. It's only two quid, and it's better than being beaten up."

The bell rang for afternoon sessions. Cameron stood up. "I'm not paying him anything," he said as he strode off.

When the bell rang for the end of lessons, and the teacher dismissed them, he gathered his things together and made for the exit that led to the side entrance of the school. Sure enough, there were Edwards and his two mates. There was also a little crowd that had turned up to see the fun. As Cameron approached the gate, Edwards stepped in front of him to block his exit.

"Ah! Mason. There's the little matter of £2 if you please."

"You're not getting anything from me," Cameron replied.

"Would you like to rethink that?" Edwards asked him.

Cameron shook his head. "Don't think so," he said and made a move towards the gateway.

"I warned you," Edwards almost snarled, and he turned to the lad on his right. "Adams, sort him out."

Adams started to move menacingly towards Cameron, who quietly said, "Just a moment; let me put my bag down."

Chapter: 14

Adams was so surprised by Cameron's response that he stopped in his tracks for a moment whilst Cameron took his bag off, and it was only then that he made a lunge at Cameron. Cameron did a neat sidestep, ducked slightly, then stood straight up, putting his shoulder into Adams lower chest. Using the lad's own momentum, he threw him into the air so that he landed on his back and lay there winded. There were gasps of astonishment from the little crowd.

Edwards didn't look at all happy with this turn of events. He turned to the lad on his left.

"Well, what you waiting for, Watson? You sort him out." Watson suddenly didn't look too keen to be involved.

"If you want your two quid, get it yourself. This guy looks as though he knows what he's doing."

Edwards now had a dilemma. Everyone was watching him to see what he was going to do now, and the crowd had got a little bigger. He knew that if he let Cameron go, he would lose all credibility. He made his decision, took a pace forward and aimed a punch at Cameron's face. This was a big mistake; Cameron was ready for it. He caught Edwards' arm and, in a flash, had it tight up behind his back. He pushed Edwards up against the brick gatepost so that his face was pressed against the cold bricks.

"Now, say you're sorry," Cameron said in his ear, "or I'll break your arm." He pushed the arm a little further up his back to show that he meant it. "And tell your mates to move back or else...."

Edwards almost screamed, "Don't come near him."

"Now then, say you're sorry for trying to hit me and say you're sorry for taking money off this lot."

Edwards almost whispered, "Sorry."

"Not loud enough. They couldn't hear you; say it louder."

To make sure that he did, Cameron exerted a bit more pressure on the arm. Edwards said sorry this time in a much louder voice. "That's much better. Now, where's the money that you've collected off them?"

"It's in a tin in my bag."

Just then, there was a loud shout. "Mason, what's going on here?" It was Mr Buxton, one of the housemasters. "Let go of Edwards."

"I will in a moment, sir. I am just organising a re-distribution of wealth."

"What do you mean?"

"Edwards has been running a protection racket, sir, threatening all these boys. He's been charging them £2 a half term. You'll find the money in a tin in his bag."

Mr Buxton looked at the crowd of boys. "Is this true?"

Almost in unison, they replied, "Yes, sir."

"Where's his bag?" One of the boys handed it to him, and sure enough, inside there was a tin, where, when he opened it, Mr Buxton discovered £40 or £50 mostly in pound coins. All this time, Cameron had Edwards up against the gate post. "I think you can let him go now, Mason."

"Yes, sir."

Mr Buxton looked at the group. "How many of you paid Edwards money?" Hands shot up. "Right. Form a queue, and I'll pay you back, but no cheating, and you, Edwards, stay there. Don't go trying to sneak off."

There was just £3 left when all the boys had been paid off.

"Mason, we don't approve of violence at this school."

"No, sir."

Gary was quick to jump in. "Mason didn't start it, sir. He wouldn't pay up, so Edwards set Adams on him. Mason threw him over his shoulder, and then Edwards tried to hit him. He was only defending himself, sir." He turned to the rest. "That's right, isn't it?" Some nodded, and some added, "It's true, sir."

"Right, you've all got your money, now get off home. I might want to talk to some of you after half term." He turned to Edwards. "And I'll definitely want to talk to you and you, Mason."

"Yes, sir," Cameron replied.

Edwards sort of grunted, gave Cameron one last look, and skulked off, rubbing his arm. Cameron picked up his bag and started to walk away.

"Mason."

"Yes, sir."

"Don't spend half-term worrying about this," he said and smiled.

"No. sir. Thank you, sir."

Chapter: 15

When he got home, Cameron knew that he had no choice but to tell his parents everything. His mum was horrified, but his dad was quite calm about it.

"I think that you did the right thing. You need to stand up for yourself. Bullies can't be allowed to get away with things, and as long as no one got hurt, then that's OK by me just as long as the school don't punish you. Those self-defence lessons came in handy, then."

It was the topic of conversation on the Monday back after half term. A few of the boys came straight to Cameron when he walked through the school gate. Most of them just said thanks and sidled off. Gary walked with him.

"That was impressive last Friday."

"Thanks, but I don't want a fuss made or to be held up as a hero. Probably it will soon be forgotten."

"Doubt it," said Gary.

The call to go to see Mr Buxton came halfway through the morning. He knocked on the door of his office and waited.

"Come."

He opened the door and went in.

"Ah, Mason. As I said to you last Friday, we don't approve of violence, but in this case, it appears to have been completely justified. In addition, you have managed to sort out something that the school has been completely unaware of. Apparently, this racket has been going on for at least eighteen months. You'll be pleased to know that the school will not be taking any disciplinary action against you."

"Thank you, sir."

"Now, let's talk about you. I have had a word with all the staff who teach you, and they are all very happy with the standard of your work, but one or two are concerned that you seem a little isolated, withdrawn even. Are you not happy here?"

"If I'm honest, sir, no, I'm not. I had lots of friends back home. We had a youth club; we met at each other's houses. I played in a football team. It was great. We had been together a long time. I guess that there are some groups like that here. It's not deliberate on their part, but they don't really need me, so it's hard to break in."

"I could be wrong, Mason, but after last Friday, you might find it a little easier. Is there anything else that you would like to say?"

Cameron paused. "There's just one thing, sir. I won't exactly be popular with Edwards and his friends...." his voice trailed off.

"Oh. There's no need to worry about that. Their families have been warned that any other misdemeanour, including a revenge attack on yourself, either in or out of school, will be punished by expulsion. Now, if that's all, off you go. Oh, just one more thing Mason; where did you learn self-defence?"

"At the youth club, sir. One of our friends got beaten up the Christmas before last, so we asked for lessons."

Mr Buxton smiled. "Well, Cameron. That was one event that came in useful; perhaps last Friday will be just as important for you."

"Yes, sir."

At lunchtime, a few were eager to know what had happened in Mr Buxton's office.

"Not much, actually. I'm not in trouble or anything." Then their questions started. The first questions were about how he knew self-defence, but then they branched out into other things, such as what was his other school like or if he played football for a team back there.

Then Gary dropped a bombshell. "A few of us play football for Clifton Athletic Juniors. We would like you to come and join us." He looked at the others, who nodded encouragingly. "We know you are a good player."

Just then, the bell rang, and as Cameron stood up, he said, "I'll have a think about it."

Dan lived just down the road. Before that eventful Friday afternoon, he was about the only one that Cameron really spoke to. He went to the same school but was in the year below Cameron. They usually walked to the bus stop together and then sat together upstairs on the bus. Cameron realised that they didn't have too much in common, but it was nice just to chat with someone. Dan usually asked the questions and Cameron good naturedly responded. Mostly the questions were about his old school, or the youth club or life in general in the north of England. Sometimes Cameron thought that Dan seemed to think the north was a different country. *And it might as well be, as far as I and Coral are concerned,* he thought.

One other person used to get on the bus at the same stop - a rather pretty girl. And because of her school uniform, Cameron realised that she went to another school further across town. Cameron and Dan always seemed to sit in the seat behind her. She used to get off in the town centre and meet up with other girls to catch another bus. He had noticed her the very first day, and she apparently noticed him because she gave him a nice smile. He always let her get on the bus first, and because she had a name tag in the hood of her coat, he knew that she was called Penelope. Usually, there were very few passengers on the bus at this point, and she always sat by herself. The bus filled up as it got closer to town.

Chapter: 16

The Wednesday morning following half term, Dan didn't appear, so Cameron walked to the bus stop by himself. When the bus arrived, he as usual let Penelope get on first, and as she sat down, on an impulse, he spoke to her for the first time.

"Do you mind if I sit next to you?"

She looked up at him, smiled, and said, "No, and it's about time." He gave her a puzzled look.

"Well, you've been here almost two months, we meet most mornings, and this is the first time you've spoken to me."

"I'm sorry, I usually sit with Dan."

"I know that; I'm only teasing. He asks so many questions, and you patiently answer them. I feel that I already know loads about you. It's nice to meet you, Cameron. See, I already know your name, thanks to Dan."

"Do they call you Penelope or Penny?" She gave him a puzzled look. "There's a name tag in your hood." He smiled.

"Penny will do nicely. I hear that you are quite a celebrity at school at the moment."

"What do you mean?"

"I understand that you sorted out a bully the other week."

"How do you know about that? And it was nothing really."

"My best friend is Ruth, and her twin is Gary. You know Gary." He nodded. "Well, on Monday, she was full of it about how you had managed to get all the money back for them. When she said that it was a new boy at the school, I worked it out - thanks to Dan - that it was probably you. Also, you weren't on the bus before Christmas so I sort of guessed that you were new. Ruth also said that Gary and his friends had asked you to join their football team and you hadn't really answered them yet."

"I said that I'd think about it."

She looked at him. "Well, have you thought about it?"

"No, not really."

This time she smiled at him. "You should. It's a really good club, a sports club, not just a football club. Families go. My family is a member. I play hockey and tennis there."

Cameron looked at her quizzically, "Am I to take it that you are sort of trying to invite me to join this club?" She nodded.

"OK then, that might just swing it," he smiled, and then said, "You'd better get going; this is your stop." He stood up to let her off. "See you tomorrow, Cameron," she said and was gone.

When Cameron got to school, there was a little group waiting for him. "Have you decided yet?" Gary inquired.

"I'm still thinking about it. I might have just had a better offer," he said with a smile.

"Who from? Not Easton Rovers? They nearly always beat us."

"Sounds like the team to join then," laughed Cameron, walking off to the form room.

The next morning there was still no Dan, so he sat with Penny again. "Have you decided?" she asked.

"Probably…but I got them a bit worried yesterday and left them thinking that I might join Easton Rovers, whoever they are." She looked at him, her face screwed up slightly.

"Don't worry; I'd never heard of them until they mentioned them, so I told them that I might have had a better offer. They just assumed it was this other team." She laughed.

"It's football and hockey practice tonight. Why don't you come with me? Dad takes me. We'll pick you up about 6:20." There was a pause.

"OK," he replied. It was almost her stop again.

"See you later then, Cameron," and she got up and went down the stairs.

At school, they were waiting for him again. "Have you made up your mind yet?" Gary almost pleaded.

"Maybe…you'll probably know by tonight" was his reply. At every break, they were there, explaining what was so good about their club. Cameron had to admit to himself that it did sound good.

At the end of school, as he was walking through the gate, they were there again. "You said we'd probably know by tonight."

He kept walking. "And you will," he said over his shoulder.

When Cameron got home, he told his mum that he would need an early tea because he was going to football practice. She was delighted. "You really need to get out and meet people, and you love football. How did this happen?"

Explanations out of the way, tea over, homework finished, he got his kit together. Bang on 6:20, a car pulled up at the gate. Penny was halfway up the drive when he opened the door. "Bye, Mum, see you later."

Chapter: 17

"You're keen," Penny remarked.

"I was in the front room and saw the car arrive. I didn't want to keep you waiting." He got in the car, and Penny introduced him to her dad.

"Pleased to meet you, Cameron. I've heard quite a bit about you."

Cameron sighed, "All good, I hope."

"Oh yes! All good."

"That's a relief then."

It didn't take long to reach the club. Cameron was amazed by the size of it. Several football pitches, a couple of hockey pitches, a square roped off for cricket in the summer and three tennis courts. The clubhouse was just as impressive - brick built with a covered veranda. The inside, he guessed, would have several rooms in addition to the changing rooms. Cameron had never seen anything like it back home. The floodlights were on as well.

Almost as soon as the car stopped, it was surrounded by Gary and his friends. Before they could say anything, he said, "I told you that you would know by tonight."

He turned to Penny's dad. "Thanks for the lift," he said.

The little group, including Penny, headed for the clubhouse. Before they got there, they were met by a couple of girls. Cameron realised that one of them was Ruth. She was so like Gary. It was almost uncanny.

Ruth looked at Penny. "You were right," she said, then spoke to Cameron. "Hi, I'm Ruth; I'm Gary's sister…and this is Lucy."

"I think I guessed that you were Gary's sister. You're the better looking one," he replied. The others all laughed. Cameron went on, "And what was Penny right about?"

"That's between Penny and me," she answered.

Gary introduced Cameron to Joe, the football coach. "It's nice to meet you, Cameron. I've been told that you are a good player. Let's see, shall we?"

The practice went well. Cameron played in midfield and enjoyed himself. He realised that he was as good, if not better, than most of the other lads.

When the practice was over, Joe came to Cameron. "They were right," he said, "you are good. We've got a game on Saturday. I can't put you straight in the team, although I'd like to. That wouldn't be fair on the lads who have played all season, but I'll put you on the bench. Is that OK?"

"That's fine. I get what you're saying."

"Oh, and you'll need to sign a membership form and pay the fee, or you can't play." Back in the changing room, Joe announced the team for Saturday. Some seemed surprised that Cameron was only on the bench. When he was dropped off at home, he thanked Penny's dad for the lift, said goodnight, and went in.

His dad was waiting for him. "How did it go?"

"Not bad; I'm on the bench for the game on Saturday."

"I might come and watch then," his dad said.

The next day at the bus stop, there was no Dan again. Sat together again, Penny asked Cameron if he enjoyed himself the previous night.

He nodded. "What were you right about?" he asked.

"Maybe I'll tell you later." She grinned.

When he arrived at school, Gary was there to meet him and said, "We thought you'd be straight in the team."

"Don't worry about it. I didn't expect to get in straight away."

The hockey team were playing at home on Saturday as well, so he got another lift to the club. The match started, and it ebbed and flowed, but gradually, the opposition started to get the upper hand and just before halftime, they scored.

During the team talk at halftime, Joe looked at Cameron and said, "Make sure that you are warmed up. I might bring you on for the last fifteen."

Not much changed after halftime, and both teams had chances, but Joe, true to his word, sent Cameron on with about fifteen minutes to go.

He soon got involved, making a few good tackles, several important interceptions, and never misplacing a pass. There wasn't long to go when he made another interception, looked up, and saw Gary in loads of space. He played the pass, inch-perfect, and Gary blasted the ball into the net. Cue great celebrations! Shortly after that, the whistle blew.

As they were shaking hands with the opposition, Cameron looked up and saw his dad for the first time. His dad gave him the thumbs up. He also noticed that most of the hockey team were on the touchline as well. As he walked off, Joe patted him on the back. "Well played, Cameron, great pass. I might have to give you longer next time."

As Joe walked away, Penny arrived by Cameron's side.

"We watched the last ten minutes. You were great."

"Thanks, but it wasn't just me. Gary scored the goal."

Then Gary was there.

"Great pass, Cameron; you made the difference today."

113

Chapter: 18

Life for Cameron improved a little after that, especially at school, where now he felt more included. Sometimes on the bus, he sat with Dan and sometimes with Penny. He got on well with Penny, and he sensed that she really liked him. This gave him a dilemma. He knew that he was still in love with Coral, and he still missed her, especially on Friday evenings when he knew that all his old friends would be around at the Browne's. The last thing he wanted was for Penny to start thinking that they were more than just friends.

As the football season progressed, Joe gave him more and more game time. Cameron knew he should be starting the games now, but he also knew how he would feel if he had been playing from the start of the season and then someone new came along and replaced him. So far, for the time being, he was happy with things as they were. Perhaps next season, he would be in the starting line-ups.

The next to the last game of the season was the cup final. Teams reaching the final tossed for the venue, and Joe won the toss, so Clifton obviously chose to play at home. On the day, there was quite a crowd of spectators from both teams, including Cameron's mum and dad.

The hockey season was over, but some of the team had turned up to watch. Cameron noticed that Penny was there with her parents. The club had also decided that no matter what the result, afterwards they would hold a little celebration and disco in the clubhouse. The team had been told to make sure that they had a fairly decent set of clothes to change into.

The game was close, but just before halftime, Clifton took the lead.

In the dressing room, Joe gave his half time talk. "Don't go making any silly mistakes; keep calm and use our wingers. Cameron, you'll be on after about 15 minutes. We'll need your fresh legs by then."

Things didn't go according to the plan, though. After about ten minutes of the second half, Alan, the goalkeeper, was injured, and it soon became obvious that he couldn't carry on. Joe hadn't planned for such a scenario. They had no substitute keeper; no one on the bench wanted to do it.

"I'll do it then," said Cameron.

"Have you ever played in goal before?" Joe asked.

"No, but no one else is volunteering."

The change was made, and Cameron went in goal. To be fair, he didn't have too much to do as the defenders did an excellent job of keeping the opposition at bay. He was forced to make one or two routine saves and a couple of catches from corners. As his confidence grew, he started to issue instructions and encouragement, but worryingly, he sensed that Clifton was tiring. Joe made another substitution, but it didn't help much. There wasn't more than five minutes to go when Roy, the full-back, made a tired looking tackle in the area. The referee blew for a penalty, and Clifton couldn't really complain. Worse still, Roy was shown a red card.

The opposition captain put the ball on the spot. Cameron looked at him intently and caught his eye.

"Left or right, it doesn't matter," Cameron said, "I'll save it."

The kicker tried to ignore Cameron, but from the expression on his face, Cameron sensed that he had unnerved him. He also noticed that an eerie silence had descended around the ground, but now he was really concentrating on the kicker.

Suddenly, he just knew which side he was going to put it on. The referee blew. As the kick was taken, he dived to the left, and he knew that he had guessed correctly. He pushed the ball around the post and was mobbed by the team. There was wild cheering on the touchline. "Just defend this corner," he shouted. The spot miss seemed to deflate the opposition, and Clifton played out the remaining minutes comfortably. At the final whistle, the home spectators

116

dashed onto the field. The next few minutes were a blur, handshakes, hugs and thumps on the back. Not just for Cameron but for the whole team. Eventually, some sort of order was restored, and the presentations were made.

First of all, the medals for the losers, then the medals for the winners, and then finally, the cup was presented to Gary. Cue more cheering and clapping! After changing out of their kits, the celebrations got underway. His mum and dad came and sat with him. They didn't say much, but the look on their faces told him everything. After the food, Joe stood up and asked for quiet, which he got after a bit of heckling from his audience.

"There is always 'Man of the Match' award after a cup final. The president of the club, Mr Marshall, watched the whole game and is here to make the presentation. He has also chosen the 'Man of the Match,' so now, I will hand over to you, Mr President."

Mr Marshall stepped onto the stage at the front of the hall. He started to speak.

"Congratulations to the team. It's quite a while since we last won this trophy, so well done to you all. Now, normally, when a team wins a cup, the 'Man of the Match' award usually goes to the goal scorer, but on this occasion, I am going to award it to our magnificent substitute goalkeeper, Cameron Mason."

Cameron looked shocked as the room exploded in wild cheering and clapping. "Up you come, Cameron." Cameron walked to the front feeling a bit embarrassed but inwardly pleased. He shook hands with Mr Marshall and accepted the small trophy.

"Thank you." He turned to walk back to his mum and dad amid shouts of "speech." He smiled, shook his head, and said, "No chance." He gave the trophy to his mum. "You look after it, please."

Now the formalities were over; the disco started. Many of the adults drifted away. Cameron's dad said that he would come back for him later. The lights went down, and the music started. At first, he sat with a few of the team at the side, just watching. As usual, the girls were up first. Then a couple of the girls came across and dragged Gary and Roy onto the floor. The next thing Cameron knew, Ruth was in front of him. "Dance with me, Cameron." It was a bit unexpected, but he got up and danced with her for a while. When the music changed, he told her that he was a bit tired. She appeared slightly disappointed but nodded, and so he went and sat down again. The next thing he knew, Penny came and sat next to him. "She fancies you," she said, "but actually, a lot of the girls do."

"Can't think why," Cameron replied.

"That's because you're not a girl." She laughed.

They sat talking for a while, then she stood up and pulled him to his feet. "Have you recovered enough for another dance?" He followed her onto the floor, which by now was quite crowded. They had been dancing for a few minutes when he noticed that Ruth was laughing and shaking her fist at Penny. Penny laughingly stuck out her tongue and noticed him watching. "See, she's jealous of me," and she tried to kiss him.

He pushed her away. "No, Penny, I can't do this. I'm sorry," and he left the floor and headed for the door. He found a bench outside and sat down with his head in his hands, and cried.

A few minutes later, Penny found him and sat down next to him. "Cameron, I'm so sorry. I thought you liked me. I didn't mean to upset you. Believe me, and I wasn't just trying to make Ruth jealous."

"I do like you Penny, I like you a lot, but the truth is I am in love with someone else."

"Who? Not Ruth?"

"No, not Ruth. She's called Coral, and she lives back home, and I miss her so much." He was still crying.

Penny put her arm around him and said, "You'd better tell me all about it."

He told her the whole story. When he had finished, he looked at her and said, "I'm sorry."

She just looked at him. "Cameron Mason, Coral, is a very, very, very lucky girl, and I'm jealous of her." There was a pause. "If you won't be my boyfriend, will you still be my friend?"

He looked up again. "If that's what you want, then yes, as long as you don't tell anyone about this, including me crying."

She pecked him on the cheek. "It's a deal. Now come back inside." When they got back inside, there was a little huddle waiting by the door.

Ruth grabbed Penny by the arm. "Is everything alright? Cameron looks a little upset."

"Everything is fine; stop worrying."

She caught Cameron up. "Come on, dance with me; that'll stop them from gossiping." She grabbed his hand and pulled him onto the floor. For the rest of the evening, Penny looked after him. She encouraged him to dance with some of the other girls when they asked, made him go and sit with the boys for a while, but always came back to rescue him when she thought the time was right.

It was Penny who spotted Cameron's dad arrive. "Your dad's here," she said. He stood up to leave. "I'll walk to the door with you," she said. He said goodnight to those near the door and asked Penny if she wanted a lift home.

"No, thanks; Dad's coming for me."

Once through the door, he turned to her, gave her a hug and whispered in her ear, "Thank you for understanding."

"Goodnight, Cameron, I'll see you on the bus on Monday." She watched him go and then turned to go back inside with tears in her eyes.

As they drove home, his dad remarked, "It's a good job. Coral didn't see that goodbye."

"Penny knows all about Coral. I told her tonight. Penny and I are friends. That's all."

When they got home, his mum asked if it had been a good night. "In the end, I think so," he said. He noticed his trophy in pride of place on the bookcase. His mum saw him looking at it.

"I'll try it in different places to see where it looks best," she said.

Chapter: 19

When they were sitting down having a drink and talking about the game, he suddenly said, "Mum, can Coral come and stay for a few days over Easter?"

She looked at him. "Cameron, love, of course, she can. I'm surprised that it's taken you so long to ask. I'll ring her mum tomorrow and see if we can sort it."

Cameron went to bed feeling happier than he had done in ages. His mum was as good as her word. She rang Mrs Browne, and between them, they agreed that Coral could come down by train a week on Friday. Mrs Mason smiled. She could hear Coral shouting in the background, "Yes please, yes please," when her mum asked her if she wanted to go and spend a few days with the Mason's.

Walking to the bus stop on the Monday, Cameron told Dan that he was going to sit with Penny because they would probably want to talk about the match. "We won the cup, one-nil," he told him.

"Well done, did you score?" asked Dan.

"No, but I saved a penalty," laughed Cameron.

Dan looked puzzled. "I thought that you played in midfield."

"I do usually, but I had to go in goal." By this time, they were at the bus stop, and Penny was there.

"All right?" she asked knowingly. He nodded. When they sat down, he told her that Coral was coming to stay for a few days at the end of next week. "That's good. You'll be happy then." He nodded again. Then she said, "The end of season party is on Saturday next week. You'll be able to bring her to that."

"Maybe," he replied. The next few days dragged for Cameron. Saturday came, and they played the last game. After the euphoria of winning the cup, the team didn't play well and ended up drawing 1-1. Even Cameron was below par, but his mind was elsewhere. Joe wasn't best pleased with them, but as they had won the cup and been runners up in the league, he admitted that it was a bit churlish to complain.

"End of season presentations and party next week," he reminded them. Don't be late. Parents are invited. Make sure that you tell them."

The last day of school was on the Thursday. When they were on the bus, Penny asked, "Well, when is she arriving?"

"Tomorrow afternoon, 2 o'clock by train."

"Who's meeting her?"

"Just me, dad's working. I'll catch the bus to the station."

"Cameron, can I come with you? I'd like to meet her before everyone else. You can say no. I would understand."

He looked at her, "Are you sure?"

She nodded, "But I don't want to upset Coral."

"Ok then, actually, I think that I would like you to meet her, and she will definitely like you."

At 1.45 pm, they were at the station waiting. Cameron was pacing up and down.

"Let's sit down, Cameron. The train's not due yet." Reluctantly he sat down, but every few seconds, he would glance at the big station clock. Just after 2 o'clock, the station announcer informed them that the train approaching platform 3 was the train from Manchester.

"Go on," said Penny, "Meet her at the barrier. I'll wait here." He didn't need a second invitation. As the train stopped, he scoured the platform, trying to catch a first glimpse of her. Then, there she was, and his heart thumped. She spotted him and waved, and when she was through the barrier, she ran towards him, dropped her case and threw herself into his arms. Their kiss was interrupted by Penny.

"I guess that you two know each other," she said laughingly. They broke off the kiss, and Coral looked a bit confused and looked at Penny, then back at Cameron.

"Coral, this is Penny, and Penny, this is Coral. But I'm sure that you've guessed that already." He turned to Coral. "Penny is a good friend; she knows all about you, and she's been good to me the last few weeks. I'll tell you about it later."

Penny responded, "It's very nice to meet you, Coral. Cameron has told me a lot about you."

"I hope it was all nice," Coral replied.

"Oh, you don't have to worry about that. It was," Penny replied. "Come on, let's get out of here," and Penny picked up the case.

"Hey, I'll carry that," said Cameron.

"No, you won't," laughed Penny, "You've got your hands full already." As they walked off, Coral and Cameron, hand in hand, Cameron looked at Coral, "See, I told you she was a good friend."

On the bus, they chatted about Coral's journey and the Presentation Evening. "Has he told you that he's taking you out tomorrow night?" Penny asked.

"Yes, and he told me to bring something nice to wear."

"I am looking forward to tomorrow," said Penny, "I think a few people are in for a big surprise." She looked at Cameron and smiled.

"Why's that?" Coral asked.

"Because you are Cameron's big secret. Apart from me, I don't think anyone at the club knows about you."

When they got to their stop, they got off. "I'll see you both tomorrow. Have fun and enjoy your time together," and Penny walked away.

Coral looked at Cameron, "She's nice. I like her."

"So do I," Cameron replied.

Mrs Mason had been watching for their arrival, and as they were halfway up the drive, she opened the door. She gave Coral a big hug, "Hello Coral, love. It's nice to see you again."

"It's nice to see you," Mrs Mason, "Thank you for inviting me." The three of them spent the remainder of the afternoon talking, and when Mr Mason returned from work, they sat down for a meal.

Later Cameron and Coral went for a walk. He told her all about the events at school. "You never mentioned any of this in your letters or phone calls."

"No," he admitted, "But it's easier to talk face to face, and I certainly couldn't have written it all down." Then he told her about the incident with Penny after the cup match. She was holding his hand, and she stopped walking, so he had to as well.

"Cameron Mason, You cried because you missed me. Oh, Cameron, I do love you," and she kissed him.

Chapter: 20

The next morning they went into town and just wandered around. Cameron hadn't been into town much himself since the move, so much of it was new to him as well. They found somewhere for a coffee and then went back in time for lunch. Afterwards, Mr Mason asked if they would like to visit the zoo. Naturally, Coral was enthusiastic about the idea, so the four of them spent a happy couple of hours looking at all the animals and, in particular, laughing at the monkeys. Mrs Mason noticed that in all that time they were there, Coral and Cameron hardly let go of each other. She was also acutely aware that she had not seen Cameron so happy for ages. She said as much to her husband. He admitted that he had noticed that as well.

Back home, after a snack, it was time to get ready for the presentation evening. When it was time to leave, Coral seemed to take ages to appear, but when she did, she looked gorgeous. She just had a hint of make-up, and she was dressed in a light blue blouse with a dark blue skirt and black low heeled shoes. And she was wearing the earrings that Cameron had bought her for the Christmas before last, and around her neck, Cameron could see the locket.

Mr Mason was the first to speak. "You look lovely, Coral. Say something, Cameron."

Cameron had always known that Coral was a pretty girl, but seeing her now, he thought that she was prettier than ever, and he was almost speechless. "You look beautiful," he said.

"Thank you," she smiled at him. Mrs Mason stepped forward and hugged her.

"Cameron is so lucky to have you, love," she whispered in her ear.

When they got to the club, it was obvious that most people were already there. The car park was almost full. Mrs Mason said, "Your dad and I will go in first. I want to see the reaction when you two walk-in together." They quickly disappeared inside before Cameron could say anything.

"Come on," he said, and he took her hand, and they walked through the door together. Inside, the room was almost full, but he could see some members of the football and hockey teams over on the far side. Matthew was the first to notice them as they started to walk across the floor, and he nudged the two lads on either side of him.

"Well! Just look at this," he said. As they got closer, all the little conversations that had been going on gradually stopped, as one by one, the youngsters noticed them.

Gary was the quickest to react. He stood up.

"Cameron, you've kept this quiet." He turned to Coral, "Hi, I'm Gary, pleased to meet you." He looked at Cameron.

"This is Coral, my girlfriend from back home." Then they were surrounded by the group, all anxious to be introduced. Matthew found two extra chairs so that they could sit down. Coral was the centre of attention for a few minutes, and while all this was happening, he noticed Penny looking at him. He caught her gaze, and she smiled at him and gave him a little 'thumbs up'.

When the commotion was over, and he was sat next to Coral, he put his arm around her and pulled her close. A few minutes later, the presentations started.

The hockey teams were first. There were medals for the players in the successful 2nd Team and Player of the Season trophies for 2nd Team and 1st Team.

Then it was on to the football teams. First, there was a Player of the Season trophy for the 2nd X1. Then there was a trophy for the 2nd X1 Player of the season chosen by the players.

Then it was on to the 1st X1. The Player of the Season chosen by the manager was Gary. After receiving his trophy, Gary stayed at the front and explained that the player of the season chosen by the players was done by secret ballot. "This season," he went on, "We had a very odd situation. It's never happened before. Every player, except one, voted for the same person. The players' 'Player of the Year' is," and he paused, "Cameron Mason." The room burst out in applause. Cameron was genuinely shocked. He looked around at the others.

"Are you sure?" They were all smiling and nodding. Roy started pushing him.

"Get up there and collect it." Cameron made his way to the front and collected his trophy from Joe.

"Thank you, this is a surprise," and he turned to go back to his seat. Cries of "Speech" were heard. He smiled. "No chance," he said and went and sat down.

Coral snuggled in to him and whispered into his ear, "Well done. I wonder who didn't vote for you."

"That would be me. You can't vote for yourself. I voted for Gary."

The food was available, and as they sat around, people came up to talk and congratulate him. It soon became obvious that the moment he saved the penalty was the moment that everyone in the team decided to vote for him. He went across to his mum and dad and gave the trophy to his mum. He could tell that they were pleased. His dad never said much, but this time he just said, "Well done, son."

Later, the music started quietly at first, so everyone could talk. He noticed that Coral was now chatting easily with the girls and occasionally with the boys. Then some started to get up and dance. Gary came to him. "Can I ask Coral to dance?"

"Yes. Why not?"

Gary went across to Coral, who was sitting with Penny and Ruth. Cameron could see him ask, and she stood up straight away. That was the cue for Ruth. She was across to Cameron like a shot. She smiled, "Player of the Season, will you dance with me? You can't be tired tonight!" The evening was going well. Cameron was happy.

Coral came and sat next to him. "They are nice," she said, "and the boys are behaving like gentlemen."

"They don't always," he laughed, "You should hear them on the football pitch sometimes." Towards the end of the evening, the DJ put on a Beatles Medley. Nearly everyone was up now. Cameron and Coral were together on the floor for almost the first time. The last song in the Medley was the nice and slow 'And I Love Her'.

Coral had her arms wrapped around him, and they were gazing into each other's eyes. He started to kiss her. It was Coral that sensed it first. "Everyone is watching us."

"I don't care," he said, and he kissed her again. As the song came to an end, he quietly joined in the last line, but loud enough for most to hear "And I Love Her."

The song stopped. There was a deadly silence.

Gary shouted, "I think we've worked that out, Cameron," and everyone started laughing and clapping.

Ruth and Penny had been watching. "How do you compete with that?" Ruth asked.

"You can't, and anyway, it's not a competition. Just be happy for them," Penny replied.

"You knew about her, didn't you?" Ruth went on.

"What makes you say that?"

"I think that apart from his mum and dad, you were the only one who wasn't surprised when they walked in. How long have you known?"

"Since cup final day," Penny replied.

Ruth nodded. "I get it now. He told you while you were outside. I knew he was upset. I knew that something was wrong."

"Well, it's right now," smiled Penny.

Cameron led Coral off the floor, and they sat together. She had her head on his shoulder. "That was lovely, Cameron. Say it again." He turned and whispered in her ear, "And I Love Her." She smiled and whispered back, "And I Love Him," and she kissed him on the cheek.

They were on the floor again for the last dance of the evening, and then it was time to leave. Cameron and Coral walked across to the corner where they had spent most of the evening.

"We are off now," said Cameron, and he nodded to where his parents were waiting for them.

Gary stood up. "Coral, it was lovely to meet you. I hope that we see you again." The others were nodding in agreement, and a couple of the girls gave her a hug. Ruth whispered in her ear, "You lucky girl, look after him."

"Oh, I will, don't you worry about that," Coral answered with a smile.

Once in the car, Mrs Mason laughingly commented, "Well, we don't need to ask if you two had a good time tonight."

Coral looked at Cameron. "I had a lovely time," and she smiled at him. "So did I," Cameron responded, and he took hold of her hand and squeezed it gently.

The next few days passed really quickly. On the day before she was due to go home, Mr Mason asked what they would like to do. Cameron said that he didn't mind. Mr Mason looked at Coral.

"What would you like to do, Coral? It's going to be a nice day. It would be a shame to waste it."

"Is it far to the Safari Park?" she asked.

"Not really, just over an hour. Is that what you want to do?" She nodded, "Yes, please."

"Let's get going then," he replied.

As they drove through the park and saw all the wild animals, including the lions and tigers, Cameron couldn't help noticing how much Coral was enjoying it. When they were out of the car and in the covered areas looking at the animals that were behind glass, he said to her, "You really like the animals, don't you?"

She nodded. "I'd love to be a vet in a place like this." They all enjoyed the day, which finished with a meal out. Back home, just before bedtime, Coral thanked them for a lovely time.

Mrs Mason said, "We've enjoyed having you, Coral. I'm glad you've enjoyed it. Now we have a question for you.

We have a holiday booked in Ireland during August. Would you like to come with us?" Cameron looked surprised.

"You never told me about this."

Mrs Mason looked at Coral. "Well, Coral, would you like to come with us?"

"Yes, please, but I'll have to ask mum."

"It's already sorted, love. I spoke to her yesterday. She said it was up to you, but she could guess what the answer would be."

Coral was grinning, "Yes, please, I'd love to come."

His mum spoke. "That's something to look forward to then, isn't it, Cameron?" He just sat there with a wide smile on his face and nodded. Later, upstairs, before he kissed her goodnight, he gave her his 'Player of the Season' award. "I want you to have it so that you'll never forget me."

She took it off him, "I'll keep it forever," she said, "but I'd never forget you, Cameron, even if I didn't have it."

Chapter: 21

Back at school after the holiday, Gary came straight to Cameron. "I get it now," he said.

"Get what?"

"I get why you seemed so down in the dumps when you first arrived here. You were missing Coral, weren't you?"

Cameron nodded. "Her mainly," he said, "but other things as well." "Cameron, she's lovely. I'm jealous. I'd love to have a friendship like that. A lot of the girls are gutted, though. Our Ruth is for one. She's fancied you since the first day you turned up at the club."

"I know, Penny told me," he replied.

Gary went on, "The cricket season is starting this week. Are you as good at cricket as you are at football?"

"Maybe," smiled Cameron, "You'll just have to wait and see."

"I can read you now, Cameron Mason. That sort of answer probably means that you are." Cameron smiled again.

During the summer term, Cameron started to enjoy himself a bit more. It helped that he knew that in the summer, he would be seeing Coral again, but he still missed her.

He walked into the school cricket team that turned out to have a successful season, partly because Cameron produced some really good performances as a bowler, but also because he made some useful runs with the bat. As for the Clifton Athletic Junior Cricket Team, which played on a Thursday evening, it was even more successful. He enjoyed himself when batting and made some big scores. Sometimes it was a surprise when he was out. He got a reputation for big-hitting. Even some of the men from the senior team used to leave the bar if they knew he was at the crease.

He also began to enjoy the social side of the club. Every Saturday evening, when the men's game had finished, there was often a bit of a show in the clubhouse, perhaps with a comedian, or a singer or maybe a live band. Most of the youngsters used to attend. There were times, of course, when he missed Coral, and Penny became adept at spotting when he was a bit down and would make a point of sitting with him or drag him onto the dance floor if there was a band on. Some nights, when they had been warned that the comedian was perhaps not suitable for them, Gary's mum would invite them around. The first time that occurred, Cameron politely declined the invitation. At school on the Monday afterwards, Gary told him that Ruth had demanded that the next time they were meeting at their house, Gary was to make sure that Cameron turned up. Cameron laughed, "We'll see," he said.

He did go the next time. The weather was beautiful, and the twins' parents had laid on a barbecue which started in the late afternoon. Everyone was pleased to see him, especially Ruth. She made a point of asking after Coral and when he would be seeing her next. "She's coming to Ireland with us in August," he told her. She seemed genuinely pleased for him.

"That's something for you to look forward to," she said with a smile.

Everyone was enjoying themselves, but it was a bit crowded in the garden, so it was suggested that they head to the park which was just across the road. They took a ball with them, but as it was so hot, they soon got tired and just flopped on the grass. Cameron wasn't all that surprised to find Ruth next to him, and they chatted away about nothing in particular.

He began watching a young boy, probably about five years old, kicking a ball around quite close to the lake and smiled as the youngster tried to keep the ball in the air, but without much success. His mother was not far away, playing with a toddler who she had just lifted out of the buggy.

Ruth realised what he was watching and said, "He's having fun." Cameron nodded. While they were watching, the ball bounced awkwardly and rolled into the lake, and it started to float away. Obviously, completely unaware of the danger, the youngster went after it. At first, there didn't seem to be any problem as the water barely covered his shoes.

"No!" Ruth suddenly shouted, "It goes very deep there," and as she said it, the boy slid from view. Cameron was on his feet in an instant.

He looked at Ruth. "Can you swim?" She nodded. "Come on then." He pulled her to her feet, and they dashed to the water's edge. By this time, the mother had realised what had happened and was panicking. Because of the hot weather, both Cameron and Ruth were in shorts. They kicked off their shoes and waded in until they had to swim. They got to the point where they thought that they had last seen the boy.

"Can you see him?" Ruth asked. He shook his head as he twisted around and peered into the water. Then Ruth said, "Here, I can see him."

"So can I, now." He looked at her. "An arm each, Okay?"

She nodded, and they dived under, reached him, grabbed an arm each and pulled him up to the surface. The little crowd, which by this time had gathered on the path, gave a cheer. As they swam back, Cameron said, "He's not breathing." Willing hands helped them out of the water, and they laid the boy on the grass. Cameron knelt next to him.

"Ruth, kneel opposite me and support his neck." She looked at him, and without question, did as she was told. Cameron tilted the boy's head back slightly and opened his mouth, checked that the mouth was empty and began mouth to mouth. He looked up at the mother, who was watching with her hand across her mouth and tears in her eyes. "What's his name?"

"Sam," she replied.

Cameron tried again, just as he had been taught with the dummy at the youth club. "Come on, Sam, wake up," he pleaded. Ruth was watching him. He looked at her. She could see in his eyes that he was getting really worried.

"Again, Cameron, I know that you can do it." He tried again and then again, and this time the eyelids fluttered. There was a sort of gurgling noise, water spewed out of the boy's mouth, and then he was breathing.

Ruth was smiling. "Cameron, I knew you could do it. I could kiss you," she said.

He smiled back at her. "Maybe just this once," he replied.

For the next few minutes, everything was confusing. The mother couldn't stop thanking them. People were clapping them. Sam was sitting up now, wondering about all the fuss.

He was still concerned about his ball, which by this time was way out in the middle of the lake. "We'll get another ball, Sam," his mum said as she held him tight.

"The water isn't very clean. You should get him checked over at the hospital," Cameron told her. It was Gary that intervened.

"Come on, you two. We need to get you home and dried off." Ruth looked at Cameron, "Just this once," she said, and she kissed him.

Back at the house, Gary's mum took over. "Now, you two. In the shower first, and then we'll find Cameron some dry clothes." She looked at Ruth, who had a big smile on her face. "I meant one at a time in the shower, Ruth."

"Aw, mum, you're a spoilsport."

Later, when everything had settled down, Alan asked, "Where did you learn to do mouth to mouth, Cam?"

Before he could answer, Gary butted in. "I bet it was at that youth club, back home."

Cameron nodded. "Everyone should learn a bit of first aid. The last time I did that was on a dummy that had no legs." There was laughter. "I never expected to have to use it, though."

"Well, it's a good job that you were taught it," said Ruth's mum. "Well done you. And I'm proud of Ruth as well." There was a little ripple of applause.

A little afterwards, Cameron said, "I think that I should be going now," and he stood up to leave.

"I'll drive you, Cameron," Mrs Webster said, "and don't argue with me." The look on her face was enough for him to say, "OK. Thank you."

On the drive across, Cameron was very quiet. "What are you thinking Cameron'," She enquired.

"I was just wondering what would have happened if we hadn't found him in the water, and what if we hadn't managed to start him breathing again?" She noticed that he said 'we' not 'I'. "Don't think like that, Cameron. Everything turned out fine. That's all that matters. Here we are."

"Thanks for the lift, Mrs Webster."

He was getting out of the car when she said, "I think that perhaps I should speak to your mum and dad and explain why you are wearing some of Gary's clothes and why yours are all wet and in a plastic bag."

"There's no need, Mrs Webster, I'll tell them."

"No, Cameron, I'll tell them. I'm beginning to get to know you. You don't like a fuss. You'll probably gloss over it. They need to know the full story," and she got out of the car as well.

After she had gone, his mum did make a fuss, and the following week the fuss got even worse. First, at the bus stop on the Monday morning, Penny greeted him, "What's it like to be a hero?"

He looked at her. "Who told you? Oh! Let me guess, Ruth."

She nodded. "I saw her yesterday."

"It was nothing really, and two of us did it. Ruth was just as involved." "It wasn't 'nothing', Cameron. You saved the boy's life." Then she smiled. "Ruth said that it was scary, especially at first, when you couldn't get him to start breathing again, but then the best bit was after it was all over, you let her give you a kiss, BUT she did stress that you said, 'Just this once',"

He smiled at that. "Yes, but just THAT once."

When he got to school, it was all over the school as well. Quite a few of the boys made a point of congratulating him. Halfway through the morning, he was summoned to Mr Buxton's office. He knocked on the door and waited. "Come in. Ah Cameron, sit down." Cameron, not Mason, Cameron noted. "You had an interesting weekend, I believe." "Yes, sir, I suppose I did, but how do you know about it?"

"News travels fast, Cameron. Before we go any further, I would just like to say, well done."

"Thank you, sir, but there were two of us involved. It wasn't just me. I couldn't have done it without Ruth; that's Gary's twin sister."

"You don't really like the limelight, do you?"

"No, sir."

"Well, I am afraid it's going to get worse for you. The local paper has got wind of it and wants to come and interview you." Cameron sighed. "I don't really want that sort of fuss, sir, and will they be talking to Ruth as well?"

"I don't think so. They want to come to school to do it today and take some photos."

Cameron shook his head. "No, sir. I'm sorry. I'll not do it unless they are prepared to talk to Ruth as well. We did it together. It was Ruth that actually spotted Sam first, and we both dived down to reach him. She did just as much as me."

Mr Buxton was studying him intently. "Is that your last word on the subject Cameron?" Cameron nodded. "Very well, I'll tell the press of your decision." Cameron nodded again. Mr Buxton continued, "You must think a lot of Ruth."

"I do, sir, but before you get the wrong impression, she's a friend, not my girlfriend. Coral is my girlfriend, and she's back home."

Mr Buxton smiled, "So you still think of the north as home, even though you've been here six months or so."

Cameron nodded, "It'll always be home, sir. I don't think that will ever change."

At lunch, Gary asked what had happened with Mr Buxton. Cameron told him that Mr Buxton had said that the press wanted to talk to him, but as Ruth had done just as much as him, he wouldn't do it unless they talked to both of them.

That evening, the phone rang, and his mum answered it. "Cameron, it's for you." He took the phone off her. It was Ruth.

"Gary has told me about the paper wanting to talk to you about Saturday."

"Yes, that's right, and I said that I wouldn't do it unless they were going to talk to you as well. You did just as much as me. I couldn't have done any of it without you, so hopefully, that's the end of it."

146

There was silence at the other end. "Ruth, are you still there?"

"I'm still here, and it's not the end of it. There's a reporter and a photographer sitting in our lounge right now."

"That's fine then. You talk to them then. I don't mind." There was another pause, and Cameron could hear voices in the background.

"Cameron, they really want to talk to both of us and take pictures of us where it happened. Mum says that she'll come for you." Cameron groaned. He really didn't want all this, but he couldn't see a way out of it.

"Alright then."

It wasn't as bad as he thought. The reporter was very pleasant and, much to Cameron's surprise, young and attractive. Not at all like the stereotypes that you see in films or on TV. She asked sensible questions and made lots of notes. Then they moved to the park to take the photos, a couple of them as individuals and then together. They stood side by side at the water's edge.

The photographer said, "Cameron. Put your arm around Ruth." Cameron shook his head.

"No. Sorry. I can't do that."

"Hold her hand then." Cameron shook his head again.

"Why not?"

"Because she's a friend, not my girlfriend. I'll stand close to her, but that's all."

The photographer persisted, "It's only for a photograph Cameron, come on."

Ruth butted in, "His girlfriend is my friend, and we are not going to upset her with a staged photo and then have you making up a story about us. You can call us best friends, but nothing more than that. It's side by side or nothing." So side by side, it was.

The reporter and the photographer had got want they wanted and left Ruth and Cameron together.

"Thank you," Cameron said.

"For what," she replied.

He smiled, "For being my best friend and backing me up."

"I suppose that I'll just have to make do with best friend, but I'll settle for that," she said with a grin.

Later in the week, when the paper was published, it wasn't as bad as Cameron feared. The headline read 'Best friends save toddler from drowning'. The whole story was there with pictures of them as well as pictures of Sam and his mum, who was quoted as saying that Ruth and Cameron were heroes. Of course, it did stir things up again at school, and he got a bit of good-natured banter about being a hero, but the attention soon died away, much to his relief.

Chapter: 22

The summer holiday arrived, and the Mason family made preparations for the trip to Ireland. They were travelling on the late Saturday Ferry from Fishguard, but Coral came down a few days earlier. It meant that she was able to go and watch him play cricket on the Thursday evening. Everyone was pleased to see her.

Matthew was laughing as he said, "So, he's dragged you along to watch the cricket."

"Not really," she replied, "I nearly always went to watch him when he was playing for Canalside; that's the club back home." Ruth came and sat beside her.

"I suppose he's told you about our little adventure the other week." Coral nodded.

"He sent me the paper cutting. It must have been a bit scary."

"It was. Trying to find Sam in the water and then getting him back to the bank was the easy bit. The scary bit was when Cameron couldn't get him to start breathing. At one point, I think he thought that it wasn't going to work. He looked really worried. Then suddenly, it did. When Sam started breathing, did he tell you that I said I could kiss him?"

Coral nodded. "He told me, and he also told me that he said you could 'Just this once'."

"I did kiss him, you know," Ruth said with a laugh.

"I know, he told me that as well, but I forgive you," and they both laughed. They were so busy talking that they didn't notice Cameron go out to bat, but they saw him coming back a few minutes later. "How many did you score?" Ruth asked.

"Not many," he replied.

"How many?" Ruth demanded.

"If you must know, I got one."

"Not the hero today then," Ruth replied with a smile.

"He's still my hero," Coral laughed, and she blew him a kiss.

The drive across to Fishguard took about three hours. Then it was just a case of boarding and finding somewhere to sit for the crossing. They found seats that reclined and so were able to doze occasionally. It reminded Cameron of the crossing to France the previous year, except that they couldn't see much as it was dark. They arrived in Rosslare in the early morning and drove west. They found somewhere to stop for breakfast. It was a small cottage, with just a few tables. The food was lovely.

"It was just like having breakfast in someone's front room," Coral commented later. The rest of the drive across to the west coast took them through some beautiful countryside. They had hired a house in Lahinch, and as they drove into the town, the tide was out, and they could see the wide bay and the vast expanse of beach. It didn't take long to find their house. The directions were easy to follow. It was at the end of a road that went slightly uphill, and to Cameron, it looked fairly new. It was double-fronted and larger than he had expected. Once inside, they discovered that there were great views of the beach from all the rooms at the front.

Later they went out to explore the town. In truth, it was quite a small place with a few restaurants, pubs and souvenir shops, so it didn't take long, and they headed for the beach. The tide had turned now, and Cameron and Coral were walking along the water's edge, carrying their shoes. They stopped, faced the sea and waited to see how long it was before the sea started to cover their feet. Coral got hold of his hand.

"Do you remember the last time we sort of did this?" she asked.

He nodded. "I remember," he replied, "and I remember what I asked you, and I meant it then, and nothing has changed."

She squeezed his hand. "Good!" and she kissed him. They turned away from the sea and, holding hands, walked back up the beach to where his parents had found a bench. Mrs Mason had been watching them.

She turned to her husband. "Just look at them. Don't they look happy?"

His dad nodded. "They do, and Cameron is like a different person when she is around. It makes me feel a bit guilty that we had to move away and split them up."

"I shouldn't worry too much." His mum said quietly, "I have a feeling that they will always be together."

"Are you happy, Coral," his mum asked when they reached them. She gave a big beaming smile and nodded.

"Yes, thank you, I'm very happy," and looking at Cameron, she gave his hand another squeeze.

It had been a long day, and no one felt like going out after the evening meal. Cameron had brought his CD player and a few discs, so he and Coral went into the other room to listen to music. They were sitting at opposite ends of a large settee.

"Cameron," he looked at her, "Can I ask you something?"

He nodded. There was a pause. "Go on, ask me."

"Well, we've been together ages now, and well, you've never tried to touch me."

"I touch you all the time," he replied.

"I know you do, but I didn't mean like that!"

A look of understanding flashed across his face. "You mean, why don't I try and touch you inside your blouse or jumper?" She nodded. He continued, "Because I've heard the lads at school talking about what they've done with their girlfriends, and they see it as a bit of a joke. They boast that they've got to second base, or in some cases third base. Then very often, they end up either being dumped or dumping the girl and moving on to another. It's almost like a game to them. You're not a game to me, Coral. Just because I've not tried it doesn't mean I don't want to. I do, but I can wait."

She slid up the settee towards him and cuddled up to him. "I do love you, Cameron."

He smiled and sat up, "Just a second while I change the CD. After presentation night, I went out and bought this." He held up the 'A Hard Day's Night' CD. "I'll just find the right track." He got back on the settee just as it started to play 'And I Love Her'. "Everyone has a song, and I think that this is ours," and he kissed her on the cheek. She smiled and pulled him towards her so they could properly kiss. As the song finished, he whispered to her, "And I Love Her." "And I Love Him," was her reply.

The weather for the rest of the holiday could not have been better. They visited the 'Cliffs of Moher' and walked along the cliff path, and watched the sea crashing onto the rocks 600 feet below. The next piece of land to the west after the cliffs was America. They went to the pretty little town of Doolin and its bay and spent several hours on the cliff top, just watching a pod of dolphins put on a gymnastic display. Coral and Mrs Mason thought that it was one of the nicest things they had ever seen.

On another day, they drove to the city of Galway and used the direct route, so it only took about an hour and a half. They chose a sail up the river Corrib and then later visited the little hamlet of Claddagh. Coral noticed the distinctive Claddagh rings in several jewellers, and one shop, in particular, had a notice in the window explaining the significance of how the ring is worn. She pointed it out to Cameron. Mrs Mason was watching closely. "Which one do you like, Coral?" "They are all nice, but I do like that one."

"Come on, then love, let's go and get it for you." Coral looked at Mrs Mason.

"I can't afford it, Mrs Mason."

155

Mrs Mason smiled, "Coral, I meant that I would buy it for you." Cameron spoke up, "Mum I should be buying it for her."

"You can't afford it either; come on Coral, I mean it," and she almost dragged Coral into the shop.

Cameron and his dad were left outside. Cameron looked at his dad. "What brought that on?" he asked.

"I'm not really sure, but the other day we were talking about how well you two get on together. We were feeling a bit guilty about separating you both. I think that she might be trying to make it up to Coral, especially after reading the explanation about how to wear the ring."

Eventually, Coral and Mrs Mason emerged from the shop. Coral was smiling from ear to ear. She waved her right hand at Cameron. The ring was on her third finger, and the point of the heart was towards her wrist.

"When I wear it that way, it means someone has stolen my heart." "And I wonder who that could be," laughed Mr Mason. Coral gave Cameron a kiss and then turned to his mum.

"Thank you, thank you," and she gave Mrs Mason a hug. "I'll wear it always." Later, after exploring the rest of Galway, they found a typical Irish pub just off the main drag.

It had an extensive menu, so they stayed and had an evening meal.

The remainder of the holiday passed quickly. There was so much to see. They were particularly fascinated by 'The Burren' with its barren limestone landscape and the number of derelict castles that were dotted around. In the evenings, Coral and Cameron usually went for a stroll along the beach, and later, back at the house, they would sit in the other room playing CDs. Cameron had realised that on The Beatles CD, there was another song that seemed appropriate to them. 'I should Have Known Better' was often played more than once during an evening. Mrs Mason smiled when the faint music drifted in from the other room, as it reminded her of her youth and Beatlemania. She knew many of the words and hummed along, much to her husband's amusement.

When the new term started, things got back to normal. Sometimes on the bus, Cameron sat with Dan, and sometimes with Penny. The football season had started, and Cameron found himself picked to start the games. He realised that his friends at the club were now almost as good as those that he had left behind, although he did miss them. In the phone calls and letters, Coral kept him updated with the latest news and gossip.

Since the incident at the park, Ruth had accepted that she would never usurp Coral in his affections and their friendship had developed in much the same way as his had with Penny. Meanwhile, Gary had become his best friend, and although Matthew was a couple of years older than the two of them, the three of them got on extremely well.

It wasn't hard to like Matthew. He was always cheerful, always ready for a laugh and a joke and was just really good company. He'd left school as soon as he was old enough and joined his dad in the family business. There were two parts to the business; a haulage company and a luxury car dealership. It was a running joke between the boys. 'Will Matthew be collected in the Jag, the Merc, the Porsche or a wagon'? It was obvious that his family were well off, but somehow their wealth was never an issue to the boys.

Matthew also had a hobby. He was passionate about photography, and he nearly always had a camera with him. He took photos of anything and everything including team photos and action shots of the club teams. They were so good that there was a whole line of them framed and hung in the clubhouse foyer, and Matthew changed them on a regular basis. He did all the developing and printing himself in a room at home that had been converted into a dark room for him. Some of the boys had been in the darkroom and reported that the room was probably as big as the main bedroom in a normal house. Matthew himself made no secret of the fact that he would like his own photography business at some point, even if it had to run alongside his work for his dad.

One morning on the bus, Penny asked Cameron if he had ever been to the theatre. He had to admit that he hadn't.

"Why do you ask?" he inquired.

"You know that English is my main subject." He nodded. "Well, there's a production of Romeo and Juliet at the theatre next week. I really should go and see it. Will you come with me?"

He thought about it for a few seconds then said, "OK. It's probably not my thing, but unless I try it, I'll never know, so yes. But are you sure that there isn't somebody else that you'd rather go with?" She shook her head.

The following Friday, they were in the theatre. It was more or less as he had imagined it would be. He had seen pictures of theatres in newspapers and on TV. However, what had surprised him was how plush it must have been when it first opened, but it was now beginning to look as if it had been built nearly a hundred years ago. There were intricate carvings and gold paint everywhere and above the centre of the auditorium was a glass dome. The upholstery had been a crimson red, but now it was faded and worn.

As far as the play was concerned, he wasn't sure what to expect. He had a vague idea of the plot, of course, but he wasn't sure that he would be able to understand the Shakespearian language. Once the performance started, though, he was able to follow it better than he thought he would, and he was fascinated by the costumes. At the interval, Penny turned to him.

"Well, what do you think," she asked.

"I'm liking it a lot better than I thought I would," he admitted. "Good, perhaps you'll come with me again then," she replied.

He smiled, "Maybe," was his answer.

When they were outside and walking back to the bus station, she linked his arm, and he didn't stop her.

"Thank you for coming, Cameron. I hope that you enjoyed it." "Surprisingly, I did. But I don't think that it's something that I could get hooked on."

She smiled, "Okay! I won't ask you again."

He looked at her. "I didn't say that I wouldn't come again. IF you asked me, then I would." As they turned a corner, they almost bumped into someone. Cameron apologised, and they stepped around him.

"Mason! It is you, isn't it?" They stopped, turned around, and Cameron found himself almost, but not quite, face to face with Edwards. His heart sank. He didn't want a confrontation out on the street, and he certainly didn't want Penny involved.

"Yes, Edwards. It's me."

"Don't look so worried, Cameron. I can call you Cameron, can't I?" Cameron nodded. "I just want to thank you." Cameron was puzzled. "What for?"

"For saving Sam's life; that little boy that you pulled out of the lake is my nephew. Sam is my sister's little boy." He held out his hand. "Shake." They shook hands.

Edwards looked at Penny. "Your boyfriend is alright. Thank you is not really enough, but it's the best I can do. BUT if either of you ever needs protection, just let me know. I'll sort it, AND it will be free." He laughed, and Cameron laughed. With that, Edwards turned away, waved over his shoulder and said, "See you around."

When he'd gone, Penny looked at Cameron. "I guess that he was the one running the protection racket." Cameron nodded. "He's huge, Cameron. How did you manage to beat him?"

"Just a bit of luck, I suppose, and he wasn't expecting me to stand up to him, so he was a bit off guard. He's not in school now. He left at the end of the year. I never saw him at school after the lake incident, but it was almost the end of term."

When they got off the bus, he walked her to her front door. "Thank you for coming with me. I hope that you weren't too bored, but I'll never know, 'cos' you are too nice to say if you were," and she smiled at him, then gave him a peck on the cheek. "Goodnight, Cameron," and she was gone.

At school on Monday, Gary was straight to him. "Ruth is not at all happy with you," he laughed.

"Why what've I done?" Gary looked at him.

"Oh! I get it. She saw Penny at hockey on Saturday, so she knows that we went to the theatre together." Gary nodded.

"Well, if Ruth had asked me to go with her to something, I might have said yes," Cameron responded, "Depending, of course, on what it was she was inviting me to."

"I'll tell her that, should I?" Gary replied.

"If you like," was all Cameron said.

Chapter: 23

There was disappointment for Coral and Cameron when they realised that their school half terms didn't coincide and they wouldn't be able to see each other again until at least Christmas. Cameron began to wonder how a meeting at Christmas was going to be arranged, but an answer presented itself when his dad announced that Uncle Ben wanted to talk business with him again and had invited them to stay with him over Christmas.

Cameron's mum liked the sound of that. "I expect that will get me out of a lot of hard work. He'll arrange for us to eat out, so no cooking or washing up!" She was right.

They travelled up a couple of days before Christmas, stopping off at the Browne's for an evening meal and a chance for the adults to catch up. It was agreed that on Boxing Day, Mr Mason and Cameron would drive across and collect Coral, and she could spend the day with the Masons and Uncle Ben. Coral thought that this was a great idea. It would be nice to meet Uncle Ben again.

As his mum had expected, Uncle Ben took them out for lunch on Christmas Day and then later in the afternoon, the buffet tea arrived. The only thing that Mrs Mason had to do was set it all out. Uncle Ben had thought of everything; even the crockery was disposable, but they did use proper cutlery.

"I can't stand plastic knives and forks," Uncle Ben stated, and so the cutlery had to be washed. To be honest, the day was quiet. They watched a bit of TV and played Monopoly for a while, but then they all got bored with that. Cameron spent an hour or so playing with the model railway, but if he was honest, the time was dragging. Tomorrow couldn't come fast enough.

In the morning, just as they were about to go and collect Coral, Uncle Ben called Cameron back.

"Tell her to bring some nightclothes. If her parents allow it, she can stay for the night. It means you can have a longer time together." When he got in the car, his dad asked what his Uncle had wanted. Cameron told him and said, "If it was up to Coral, I know what she would say, but it's up to her mum and dad."

"I think it will be fine," his dad said. "And from my point of view, it will mean less driving today."

Coral was ecstatic at the news. She looked longingly at her mum, who in turn looked at her husband. He knew that he couldn't disappoint Coral, so he nodded, and Coral gave him a big hug.

"Thanks, dad."

When they got back, it seemed as though Uncle Ben had been watching for their arrival. By the time Cameron and Coral had reached the top step, the door opened, and Uncle Ben was there. As had happened the first time they met, Uncle Ben took Coral's hand and kissed her on the fingers.

"It's so nice to see you again, Coral. Have you had a nice Christmas so far?"

Before she could answer, he noticed Cameron's dad carrying her suitcase up the steps.

"You are staying over then. Excellent!"

When he paused, Coral answered him. "Thank you for inviting me, and yes, I've had a lovely Christmas."

He looked at Cameron. "Take the case off your dad and show Coral to her room." He winked at him, "And then WHEN you are ready, we'll see you down here."

As soon as they were in the room, Cameron dropped the case and then held Coral tight before giving her a kiss. "It's been ages," he said, "since the last time we were really together."

"That was just after Ireland," she replied, "Almost 130 days." He looked at her. "I keep count," she said and kissed him.

"Well, we have a whole day now, thanks to Uncle Ben and your mum and dad."

They kissed again. "I've really missed you, Coral."

She kissed him. "And I've really missed you. But I think that we'd better go down before they miss us."

Back downstairs, Coral had to tell Uncle Ben all about what she'd been doing since the last time they met. She went into some detail about her mornings at the surgery. "When I went for the interview, Hannah said that she would review the arrangement after two months, but when the two months were up, she never mentioned it. So, I didn't mention it either."

"In that case," said Uncle Ben, "you can take it that she is happy with what you are doing. I was going to ask if you still wanted to be a vet, but the answer is obvious. Now coats on. Let's go and get something to eat."

Just like the first time, Uncle Ben made Coral sit next to him, so Cameron made sure that he sat on the other side of her. Cameron realised what his dad meant when he said Ben was a 'ladies' man. He and Coral got on really well. They chatted about all sorts of subjects and laughed a lot together. After the meal, as it was a nice sunny winter's afternoon, they all went for a stroll along the promenade. Uncle Ben was not quite as nimble as he used to be, so Cameron's mum and dad ambled along with him whilst Coral and Cameron walked on ahead. Sometimes they were holding hands, sometimes Coral had linked him, and they could often be heard laughing. Uncle Ben turned to Mrs Mason, and he nodded towards the young couple,

"A match made in heaven, I think."

"Oh, I do hope so," she replied. "I do hope so."

So far, their parents were true to their word and tried to arrange for them to visit each other as often as possible. Their half terms in February did match up, and Cameron went and stayed with the Browne's for a few days. At every opportunity, they went off together, and Mrs Browne made sure that she hosted the Friday Open House that week. She was pleased to see that it looked as though Cameron had never been away. There was a lot of catching up to do, which was coupled with a great deal of laughter.

Jenny introduced Cameron to Luke. "He lives in your house now," she told him. Cameron had heard about Luke from Coral. They shook hands.

"Nice to meet you, at last, Cameron. I've heard a lot about you from everyone." As they were all leaving at the end, Ian asked, "Will we see you tomorrow at the club, Cameron?" Cameron shook his head. "No. Sadly I've got to travel back tomorrow afternoon."

167

"Oh. No."

There were groans of disappointment. Cameron continued, "It would have been nice to see everyone again. Next time I'm up, perhaps I can manage it." There were nods of agreement. The boys shook hands, and the girls gave him hugs.

Jenny whispered in his ear, "Coral is not the only one who misses you. We all do."

Easter presented him with a dilemma. Joe had arranged for the football club to go on a mini-tour of Holland. They would be away for nine days, almost all of the school holiday. When he told Coral, she said it was too good a chance to miss. When would he get another chance to go to Holland, and if he didn't go, he would be letting the team down. Reluctantly, he decided to go, much to the delight of the rest of the team. He consoled himself with the thought that Easter was late that year, so it would be a short half term to the mid-term holiday.

Chapter: 24

The tour went really well. They played three games against teams from around Amsterdam. They won two but lost the third one. Cameron enjoyed the games, particularly as he knew that he had played well and scored two goals, although one of them was in the game that they lost. Joe announced that he was pleased with them and was looking forward to managing them in the new season. Between the games, they had time to do a bit of sightseeing and one afternoon, they took the obligatory canal trip. There was also some time for a bit of shopping, and Cameron, like almost everyone else, bought a pair of decorated clogs.

As he was leaving the shop, Gary sidled up to him. "I can't possibly guess who they might be for." Cameron just smiled.

At the bus stop on the first day of the new term, Penny spoke to Dan.

"Do you mind if Cameron sits next to me this morning?" Dan shook his head. When they sat down, Penny said, "I've got something to tell you." Cameron looked at her and realised from her expression that he was about to be told something important.

"Go on," he said.

"We're moving."

"Where to?" he asked.

"Brussels," she replied. There was a slight pause whilst he took it in. "Brussels?" She nodded. "That's a surprise. How did this come about, and when is it going to happen?"

"Dad works for the government, and he is being transferred there, and we'll be leaving at the end of this half-term." Cameron went quiet. "Say something, Cameron," she said.

"I never expected that," he replied, "and I'll really miss you. I don't know what else to say."

"I'll miss you too," she said, "We've been friends for a long time now."

He nodded, "Best friends, I'd say. You were really good to me when I first came here. I will miss you."

The news spread rapidly around the club, and everyone agreed that they should hold a leaving party. It was arranged for the first Saturday of the half term. Cameron hoped that Coral would be able to come down on the Friday after school or early on the Saturday morning.

In the meantime, he wanted to thank Penny for the way she had looked after him when he first arrived. Before he arranged anything, he checked with Coral that she wouldn't mind what he planned to do. He needn't have worried. Coral thought that it was a lovely idea. After a match at the club, about two weeks before the half-term, he took Penny aside.

"If I invited you out for dinner next Saturday, just us two, would you come? It's a kind of thank you for looking after me when I was really down."

The smile on her face told him the answer. "Of course I would. That would be lovely. Thank you."

They had a lovely time. Penny looked gorgeous. The meal was excellent, and later in the restaurant lounge, they talked and laughed together. She sat up close to him, and Cameron knew that if it wasn't for Coral, he and Penny would have been more than just friends. It was getting late, and they were getting ready to leave when she whispered in his ear,

"Cameron, I've had a lovely time. You know that I'm in love with you, don't you?"

He nodded. He looked at her. "If I wasn't in love with Coral, I could easily fall in love with you."

"Do you really mean that?" she asked. He nodded again.

"Cameron, Can I kiss you?" He smiled.

"Just this once," he replied. Outside on the way to the bus, she linked him as she had done the night they left the

171

theatre, and he didn't object. At her front door, she turned to face him.

"I've had a lovely evening, perhaps one of the best ever. I'll never forget you, Cameron."

She laughed, "Now…Just this once," and she kissed him. "Good night Cameron," and she turned and dashed inside.

He met Coral at the station late on the Friday evening. His dad had driven him there and was now waiting for them in the car park. Mr Mason saw them come out of the station, already hand in hand with Cameron carrying her case. She got in the car whilst Cameron put the case in the boot. "It's lovely to see you again, Coral. It's been a while now."

She laughed. "It's 96 days since I last saw Cameron." His dad smiled, "You keep count?" She nodded. When Cameron got in the car, his dad said,

"How many days is it since you last saw Coral?"

"I don't know exactly, but it's probably close to 100."

"I know exactly," his dad replied, "It's 96 days. Somebody has just told me."

The following morning they went into town together and chose a pair of earrings as a gift for Penny. At the party in the evening, when they handed them over, it was Coral who spoke.

172

"They are from both of us," she said, "It's a thank you for being so nice to him when he first moved here."

"Believe me, Coral. It wasn't hard. Cameron is a lovely guy. You are lucky to have him. All the girls here are jealous of you, including me!" She gave Coral a big hug and kissed Cameron on the cheek. "Now, let's enjoy the rest of the evening together."

The evening did go well. Gary managed more than once to dance with Coral, but several other members of the team butted in to dance with her as well. Meanwhile, Penny and Cameron spent a lot of time together, but occasionally Ruth did manage to prize him away from her. Matthew spent most of the evening clicking away with his camera. Sometimes he managed to catch people unawares, much to the amusement of those nearby who had noticed, but he also posed groups and pairs. He made sure that he got a posed one of Penny and Cameron and also one of Coral and Cameron.

Sadly though, the evening seemed to pass very quickly, and it was soon time to say the goodbyes. There was much hugging and plenty of tears, as Penny had known most of the girls (and some of the boys) for years.

Eventually, Cameron managed to get Penny on one side. "There is something I need to know," he said.

She looked slightly puzzled. "Go on. What do you need to know?"

He was smiling now. "That first night when I came to the club, Ruth said, 'You were right'. What were you right about?"

Penny was laughing now. "I'm not sure I should tell you. You'll be embarrassed."

"I'll risk it," he replied.

"Are you sure?" He nodded. "OK then, if you're sure, I'd told her that you were very good looking." There was a pause. "Now you're blushing," she laughed.

There was another pause, and then he pulled her to him, kissed her on the cheek and whispered in her ear. "You are one of the nicest girls that I've ever met and one of the prettiest, and I'll really miss you." She pulled away a little and looked up at him.

"You really mean that, don't you?" He nodded.

"I'll miss you too, so I'm going to go now before I start crying."

She turned away and went to say goodbye to Ruth and Gary. Coral was by his side in an instant.

"You'll miss her, won't you?"

"Yes, but not as much as I'll miss you when you go back home." He put his arm around her and kissed her on the cheek. They stood and watched the huddle by the door. No one wanted the night to end, but Penny took it upon herself to end it. She turned, waved goodnight and then she was gone.

Cameron and Coral were just about to head for the car park, where they knew his dad would be waiting when Ruth stopped them.

"Don't worry, Coral," she said laughingly. "Now that Penny's gone, I'll look after him for you. Penny was like a guard dog. None of the other girls could get anywhere near him; not that I think that they had any chance. You only have to see the way he looks at you to know that he absolutely adores you."

She gave Coral a hug. "I hope that we see you again soon, in the summer perhaps," and she turned away to re-join Gary.

Chapter: 25

During the next twelve months, they struggled to see each other. It was exam year, and they both knew that the exams were important. Cameron had learnt to drive, and for his 18th Birthday, Uncle Ben had given him money to buy a little car. During the October half-term, Cameron drove up to visit Uncle Ben and show off the car. He spent a couple of nights there and managed to get across and spend a night at the Browne's. As usual, Mrs Browne was delighted to see him, and they all went out for a meal. Afterwards, Cameron and Coral went for a walk. They ended up at their favourite place, under the canal bridge. "Do you remember the first time that we came here?" she asked.

He smiled and nodded. "I'll never forget it," he replied, and he pulled her to him and kissed her. "I do miss you, Coral, but when we are together, it's like we've never been apart."

She kissed him back and held him close, and then "Come on, we'd better be getting back." When they arrived back, Mrs Browne said, "I've made up the bed in the spare room, Cameron. Is that alright?"

He smiled, "Mrs Browne, I never expected anything else."

She laughed, "Coral looks disappointed, though."

"MUM! What are you trying to say?" And they all laughed.

Trying to get together at Christmas was equally difficult. The Browne's had Mr Browne's mother staying over, and Uncle Ben spent Christmas with the Mason's. However, he returned home the day after Boxing Day. In the end, Coral managed to spend two nights with the Mason's over New Year. It did mean that she managed to get to the club's New Year Party, and everyone was pleased to see her. Ruth was especially pleased as she and Coral got on together really well. After that, with exams rapidly approaching, they hardly saw each other at all.

When the exams were over, Cameron went north for a few days and stayed with Uncle Ben. It was Ben, not having seen Coral for a while, that suggested she might like to come for a stay a night or two.

"I really like your young lady," he remarked, "It would be lovely to see her again." Naturally, Coral jumped at the chance.

Her mother agreed. "No revision to do anymore. You could do with a break."

Ben was delighted to see her again. He treated her like a princess, and for that matter, Cameron like a prince. They ate out the first evening, and the next day, he suggested a day out in the lakes. The weather was beautiful, and the views were picturesque. They had lunch in Coniston and a sail on Windermere before another evening meal in Ambleside. When they got back to Ben's, Coral told him that the day was one of the best she'd had in ages.

"I'm glad that you enjoyed it. Exams are stressful, and it's good to relax afterwards."

The exam results came out in July, and as expected, Coral and Cameron passed with flying colours. Coral was immediately accepted by Edinburgh University to study veterinary science. Her parents were naturally delighted and took her out to celebrate. The only disappointment was that Cameron wasn't there to share the success. Meanwhile, Cameron had also done well and was accepted at Exeter to study chemistry.

The cricket season was well underway, and Cameron played in most of the matches. Often, after the game was over, especially if the weather was nice, the two teams would sit and chat on the pavilion veranda and share a few beers. After one game, one of the opposition noticed that Cameron was not drinking beer. Rather he was drinking orange juice.

He started to mock Cameron. "What's going on here? That's not a man's drink."

Cameron replied, "I drink what I like. I like orange juice. I don't like beer."

The guy persisted. "Have you ever tried it?"

Cameron nodded, "I've just told you. I just don't like it."

"You just need to persevere. It grows on you."

"Do you like sprouts?" Cameron asked him.

"No," was the reply.

"Have you tried them?" Cameron responded.

"Yes, but I don't like them."

Cameron shot back his reply. "You just need to persevere. They grow on you." At this, all the opposition started laughing.

Their captain spoke up. "He's got you there, Jack: Game, set and match."

Obviously, Jack had no answer, but he wasn't about to let it drop. It probably didn't help that it was Cameron who caught him out during the match. When he thought that no one was looking, he poured some vodka out of the bottle he had bought earlier into Cameron's drink. Fortunately, Matthew had spotted him.

"What did you do that for? You've just spoilt his drink."
This got everyone's attention.

Matthew warned Cameron. "He's just spiked your drink." He turned to Jack, "Get him another."

Jack replied, "It'll not do him any harm. It's only a bit of fun, and no, I won't get him another."

Matthew stood up. "I'll sort this, Cam," and he disappeared inside, only to return a few minutes later with a glass of orange and half a glass of milk. He handed the glass of orange to Cameron and poured the milk into Jack's pint.

"Hey, you've just spoilt my drink."

"It won't do you any harm, and it's only a bit of fun," Matthew replied. His teammates roared with laughter. Their captain stood up. "Time to leave, I think."

"That's two-nil to them, Jack." He came across to Cameron and Matthew and apologised for Jack's behaviour.

"Sorry about all that. If his brains were gunpowder, he wouldn't have enough to blow his hat off," and he shook hands with both of them and ushered his team away.

Towards the end of August, he was back at the Browne's for two days. He arrived late afternoon, and Mr and Mrs Browne treated them to an evening meal as a sort of celebration of their success. The following day, they drove

180

out to the local deer park and spent the afternoon just strolling, watching the deer and enjoying the views back towards the city. Cameron noticed that Coral was a bit quieter than usual but didn't think too much about it. Back at the Browne's after a meal, they went for a walk, and as usual, they ended up on the canal towpath. They walked as far as the cricket club before turning back.

Coral pulled him close. "I enjoyed watching you play cricket here. They were happy times." Cameron was a little puzzled. It seemed an odd thing to say.

"I'm always happy when I'm with you," he responded. By now, they were at their favourite spot, under the canal bridge. She stopped and turned to face him.

"Cameron, you know that I love you. Don't you?" Before he could answer, she continued, "I've always loved you, even when we were in primary school."

"I've always loved you," he replied, and he kissed her. When he pulled away, he could see that she was upset. "What's the matter?"

"I'm worried," she replied. "We've struggled to see each other over these last twelve months when we are 170 miles apart. In less than a month, you'll be in Exeter, and I'll be in Edinburgh. That's over 450 miles. You'll be there for three years, and I'm going to be in Edinburgh for five years. How are we going to manage to see each other? Everything will be new. There'll be work, and we'll meet new people. I can't see a way for us to keep together."

Cameron was shocked. "Are you breaking up with me?" he asked, "because I don't want anyone else but you. I'll wait the five years for you."

"No, Cameron, I'm not breaking up with you." She was almost crying now. "I'll wait for you as well, but at the moment, I can't see us getting together very often. But I haven't forgotten what you said to me when you told me that you were moving to Bristol."

"What did I say," he asked, but he already knew the answer, and he continued, "I said that I would come back for you. I meant it then, and I mean it now. Whatever happens, and however long it takes, I will come back for you. Kiss me." She did. "I promise you, Coral. I will come back for you."

Chapter: 26

It took Coral a while to get comfortable in Edinburgh. For a start off, apart from the holiday in Ireland and the trips to Bristol, it was the first time that she had ever been away from home without her mum and dad. She wasn't lonely. She liked most of the other students on her course, and she got on very well with Lorna.

In their free time, they hung out together and explored the city. The good thing about Edinburgh was that almost everything was within walking distance. However, one of the first things that they did was to go on one of the Edinburgh Tour Buses just to get a taste of the city. Like Coral, this was Lorna's first time away from home, but home was much closer: she was a Geordie. Sometimes, Coral had to apologise and ask her to repeat what she had said until she had tuned in to the accent. Lorna just laughed. "Don't worry, pet. It happens all the time."

The halls of residence were to the south of the city, not far from Arthur's Seat and Holyrood Park. Sometimes it was nice just to wander around the park, or to find a seat and enjoy the autumn sun; maybe do a bit of reading or just people watch. It was at times like these that she thought about Cameron and wondered how he was doing. She knew that she was going to miss him and hoped that he would miss her. She had been really happy to receive a birthday card from him. He had sent it to her address back home, and her mum had sent it on.

It soon became obvious that the Saturday mornings spent with Hannah at the surgery had paid off. She had learnt an awful lot of the basic stuff, and it showed in the early lab work and assignments. She was pleased with the marks that she got. One morning as they were leaving the lab, the tutor called her back to tell her how pleased they were with her work.

"I've re-checked your application," she told Coral, "and I now realise why you are doing so well. You've spent a great deal of time in surgery, haven't you?"

Coral agreed that she had. "Well, it's been a worthwhile experience Coral, but I think that things will get a little more difficult as you go through the course."

"I'm expecting that," Coral replied, "but it won't put me off."

"I'm glad to hear that, Coral. I hope that you continue to do well and, importantly, enjoy it. It's no good if you don't enjoy it."

It wasn't all work. A few of them would often get together and go out on the town. This was a whole new experience for Coral. Back home, her friends had never shown much interest in going out as a group, except perhaps occasionally to the cinema or maybe to a gig. The youth club and the Friday night house meetings had always been enough.

There was one place, just off the Royal Mile, that they started to favour. The DJ was good and entertaining, and quite often, there was a live band. The thing that Coral liked the most was that you didn't have to shout to make yourself heard. She enjoyed chatting and listening to the others. One of the things she discovered was that she was far less travelled than most of the group. France and Ireland was the extent of her travel, but the foreign places, some exotic, just rolled off the tongues of some of her friends.

On one occasion, when they were at the club, Sean suddenly asked, "Coral, who's the lucky boy then?" She looked puzzled. He pointed at her ring. "You're wearing a Claddagh?" She nodded.

"Yes, I am. But how did you know it was a Claddagh?"

Sean replied, "You're forgetting that I'm from Ireland, and I know what it means when it's worn like that. I noticed it during the first week, and I've never seen you without it."

The others were intrigued and pushed him for an explanation that was duly forthcoming.

"Well, there are a number of ways to wear a Claddagh ring and each option has a different meaning.

On the right hand: - Heart pointing inward…..means in a relationship

On the right hand: - Heart pointing outward…..means you're single

On the left hand: - Heart pointing inward…….. means you're married

On the left hand: - Heart pointing outward……. Means you're engaged."

When he had finished the explanation with all the possible Claddagh permutations, he persisted. "So Coral, who's the lucky boy?"

She smiled, "He's called Cameron, and I'm really the lucky one because he's promised to wait for me to finish here."

It was then that the questions started. How long had they been together? Where is he? Had she got a picture? There was general astonishment when she said that they had been together since at least year eight, and she had been in love with him for as long as she could remember. She opened the locket. Lorna took one look.

"Coral, you've hit the jackpot there. He's gorgeous. When was that taken?"

"On holiday in France when we were almost 16. He gave me the locket when the family moved away. We've managed to stay together all this time, even though he was in Bristol and I was in Manchester. Our parents were very supportive. We went and stayed with each other during holidays, and it was on a holiday to Ireland that I got this ring. His mum bought it for me. That's how great our parents have been."

"So none of us boys has got a hope then," laughed Sean.

She smiled, "No, Sean, I'm afraid that you haven't, nice as you all are."

Sean looked across at Craig. "I did warn you, Craig." He turned to Coral and laughingly said, "You've just broken his heart, Coral. He's talked incessantly about you since the first day of term."

Craig looked a bit sheepish. "You didn't have to tell everyone," he muttered. Coral felt a bit sorry for him.

"We can still be friends, Craig, just as long as you realise that it will always be Cameron for me." He just nodded, but they could tell that he had wanted more than 'just friends'.

To ease the situation, Lorna asked, "So when will you see Cameron again?"

"Hopefully, over Christmas, or maybe New Year up here, but we've already agreed that it might be difficult."

Chapter: 27

Cameron settled quite well in Exeter. One advantage was that it was just under two hours back to Bristol, so every now and then, he made himself available to play football for Clifton Athletic. Before he left for university, the team had looked at the new fixture list and worked out which games it would be useful for him to get back for. Luckily, it looked as if one of the more important games fell the day before his birthday.

"I'll definitely try and get back for that one," he said. The team that had played together for so long had been broken up a little because of departures to universities. Unlike Cameron, not all of them could get back. On the few weekends that he was back, it was good to catch up with his friends at the club. Ruth, who was at Art College, was always glad to see him, as were Matthew and Gary.

Matthew now had his own photographic business, which was something that he had always wanted. His main source of income came from his contract with a company that specialised in taking class, team and pupil photographs in schools and colleges. However, he also had a studio and was often booked to take family photos for various family celebrations. Meanwhile, Gary was studying engineering at Bath University and usually returned home at the weekend.

189

Cameron's first lecture was interesting. It only lasted about an hour, during which the students were introduced to the staff and given a tour of the chemistry department. The head of chemistry was Professor Fitzpatrick. He told them that they were to address him as professor until he had decided whether he liked them or not. After that, if he liked them, he would allow them to call him Fitz. This brought a smile to the faces of most of the students. Then there was a mild surprise.

"I am going to pair you up for lab work. You will keep these lab partners for the whole three years unless I decide that the partnership is not working. I've looked at your applications and your background when making up these partnerships, and I've tried to make them as diverse as possible. So if you come from a rural location, you could well be paired with someone from a city or large town. When I've finished reading out the partnerships, I want you to find your partner, introduce yourselves and then go off and get a coffee together and find out about each other. I'll see you all back here tomorrow at 10.00 am."

Cameron listened to the list of the partnerships. He was beginning to wonder if his name was there, then out it came, after Susanna Butcher. When the professor had finished, he left them to find their partners. Surprisingly, it didn't take long. Some students resorted to shouting names in the hope of attracting attention; others just wandered through the group asking, "Are you...?"

He watched for a while and then noticed one girl who seemed a bit overwhelmed by it all and was standing quietly on the edge of the melee. He went over to her.

"Hi, I'm Cameron. Are you by any chance, Susanna?" She gave him a smile and nodded. He shook her hand. "I'm very pleased to meet you, Susanna. Shall we get out of here and go for a coffee like the professor said." She nodded again.

He led her towards the door, and as they passed two girls, still trying to find their partners, one of them said, "Well, you've struck lucky. I wouldn't mind being stuck with him for three years."

Cameron smiled and replied, "No. I'm the lucky one. I've got Susanna," and he ushered her out of the room.

Over coffee, they told each other about themselves. The professor had been true to his word. Susanna came from a very small village in East Anglia. She admitted that this was about the first time she had ever been so far from home, and she wasn't sure that she was going to enjoy it.

"Don't worry," Cameron told her. "I'll look after you." She looked relieved at that. "We've got all day. Let's go into town and get some lunch. I'll treat you."

She grinned. "I think she was right. I have struck lucky. Thank you."

Cameron and Susanna did get on well together, they usually sat together in lectures, and because they had to work together in the lab, they spent a lot of time together recording results and checking the work of each other. It wasn't all work, though. His dad had told him to enjoy himself. "All work and no play is no good for anyone. But just make sure that you do the work," he said.

Cameron and Susanna also got on very well with a couple of the other 'lab partnerships', and at least once during the week, they would meet up at a local pub, and at the weekends, they sampled the clubs and, after few attempts found one that they all liked. After one of these nights out, as Cameron was escorting her back to her accommodation, she said, "Cameron, can I ask you some questions?" "Sure, go ahead," he replied.

"Do you really like me, or are you just tolerating me and being nice to me?"

He was a bit shocked. "Susanna, it's not hard to be nice to you, and yes, I really like you, but what brought this on?"

"I don't know, really. I've never had a real male friend before. Back home, all the boys that I knew were only interested in beer, farming, football and sex, and then talking about it." At this, Cameron laughed. She continued, "I've never met anyone like you before, and I'm a bit confused."

"Why, what's so confusing about me?"

"It's just that I'm not sure what is normal. We've been out a few times now, and it's obvious that Lesley and Tom, and Paula and Ollie are already more than just lab partners, and Julia has admitted that she has already slept with Greg. But you've never touched me, apart from on the back when you let me go through a door before you. So it just got me wondering whether you really did like me."

"Well, I do like you, so does that help?"

"Sort of," she replied. "But then I started thinking: 'Why hasn't he touched me? Is he gay, or has he already got a girlfriend?'"

Cameron laughed. "I'm not gay, Susanna, but yes, I do have a girlfriend. She's called Coral, and I'll tell you about her if you like."

When he had finished, he said, "So now you know, and I'll completely understand if you don't want my company anymore, apart from in the lab."

"Cameron, if it wasn't for you, I think that I would have given up the course by now and gone back home. I still want us to be friends, and now I know about Coral, I understand our relationship better. So thank you for being a good friend." She linked his arm as they walked the last few hundred yards, and he didn't try and stop her.

Chapter: 28

On the Tuesday of the next week, Cameron told Susanna that he was going home for the weekend to play football and then to meet up with a few friends at the sports club. He could see that she was a bit disappointed with that news, especially when he added that it was his birthday on Sunday. "Why don't you come with me?" he said. "Do you mean that, or are you just being nice?"

He grinned, "It'll be a nice change, and yes, I mean it."

After the morning lab session on Friday, they drove up to Bristol. Once or twice she asked. "Are you sure that your parents won't mind me coming?"

"I'm positive," he replied each time. She found his little collection of CDs that he kept in the space under the armrest.

"Can I play one?"

"Go ahead." He didn't look as she loaded the disc.

"I just love The Beatles," she said, and then he realised that she had loaded the 'Hard Day's Night' CD.

When it came to the 'And I Love Her' track, he turned to Susanna and said, "This is our song, Coral and me. We play it a lot when we are together."

They pulled up on the drive, and almost before he had turned off the engine, his mum had opened the door. He introduced Susanna. "Mum, this is my lab partner Susanna, and before you ask, she knows all about Coral, and in spite of that, she still wants to be my friend."

"It's nice to meet you, love. Come in. I'll put the kettle on." They spent a pleasant evening with his parents, and Cameron was pleased to see that as the time passed, Susanna became more and more relaxed. In the morning, they had some work to write up, and in the afternoon, whilst Cameron was playing football, Mrs Mason took her into the city.

After the football match in which Clifton won 3-1, Cameron warned his friends about Susanna. "You'll all like her. She's a really nice person but a bit insecure, and before you ask, yes, she does know about Coral."

When they walked through the door, Gary and Ruth were first to spot them. Not surprisingly, Ruth came straight to Cameron and gave him a hug and a kiss on the cheek. Cameron introduced them. "Susanna, this is Ruth, one of my best friends. Ruth, this is Susanna. She's my lab partner at uni."

Ruth took charge and introduced Susanna to the rest. She seemed a bit reticent at first, but gradually she joined in the banter. Cameron noticed that Gary was taking a great deal of interest in her. When the DJ started his set, some got up to dance. Ruth almost dragged Cameron onto the floor. Susanna commented to Gary that they seemed very close.

"They are," he said, "But not as close as our Ruth would like. I guess it was the park incident that brought them so close: although Ruth always liked him even before that."

"What was the park incident?" she asked.

He looked at her. "He hasn't told you?" She shook her head. He sighed, "Typical Cameron. I'll tell you later. Come on, dance with me." She hesitated. "Please," he almost begged.

"I'm not very good at dancing," she said, still hesitating.

"That makes two of us then," Gary replied laughingly. "Come on." He held out his hand, which she took, and followed him onto the floor. Cameron was delighted to see her up on the floor, and as time went by, it was obvious that she was starting to enjoy herself.

He had a couple of dances with her. "Having fun?" he asked.

She smiled and nodded. When she sat down, she made a point of sitting next to Gary. "So, what was the park incident?" she asked. Gary told her the whole story.

Partway through the evening, Matthew got the DJ to play 'Happy Birthday' and then presented Cameron with a present. "It's from all your friends here at Clifton," he said. By the shape of it, he could tell that it was a painting or a photo. Inside was a framed photo of him and Coral that Matthew had taken at Penny's leaving party. He just stared at it, and they could tell that it was getting to him. He looked up, "Thank you, it's great."

Ruth gave him a kiss on the cheek. "We knew that you would like it, but it was Matthew's idea."

It was almost the end of the evening, and the last dance was announced. Gary pulled Susanna onto the floor before anyone else had a chance. Ruth and Cameron were together, and she whispered in his ear, "I think Gary's in love." "I had noticed," Cameron replied.

As they were leaving, Gary came up to them. "Cameron, when you come up for my birthday, please bring Susanna with you."

Cameron looked at her. "If Susanna wants to come, I'll bring her." She smiled, "Yes, please, I'd love to come."

On the way home, he asked, "Have you had a good time?" She nodded, "It's been lovely. Your friends are really nice. It's been one of the best nights I've ever had. Thank you for inviting me to come with you."

Back in the house, he showed the photo. "Oh, it's lovely," his mum said, "and you both look so happy."

Cameron smiled, "It's a bit twee to say it, but we are always happy when we are together."

"That's true," his mum replied.

Sunday was his birthday. There were some cards to open, including one from Susanna. He saved the one with the Scottish postmark until last. They were all watching him as he opened it; he looked at the front and then the message inside.

'To MY Cameron, love always from Coral xxxxxxx'. He passed it to his mum, who put it in pride of place on the cabinet. He was quiet for a while and then said, "What's for lunch?"

"We're eating out," his dad said.

On the way back to Exeter, he asked, "Are you glad that you came?" "Cameron, I've had a wonderful weekend. I can't wait to come back for Gary's party."

He glanced at her and smiled, "So is Gary better than the boys back home?"

"Much, much better", was her response. "Now tell me about you and Ruth and the rescue in the park."

He sighed, "Did Gary tell you about that? It was a long time ago. It was nothing really." She wouldn't accept that and insisted that he told her. So he did.

A few weeks later, they were back for Gary's birthday. When Saturday afternoon came, Mrs Mason asked Susanna if she wanted to go shopping again. She shook her head. "No, thank you. I don't really understand the game, but I would like to go and watch the boys play football."

Somehow, Cameron wasn't surprised. "I'll have to leave soon, so if you come with me, you'll be standing around for a while."

"Don't worry about that," his dad chimed in. "Susanna, I'll take you nearer kick-off time and stay and watch the game myself."

When Cameron got to the club, Gary was already there. "Did Susanna come up with you?" he asked.

"She did, and what's more, she's coming to watch the game, so you'd better put in a good performance." Just before kick-off, Susanna and his dad arrived. In truth, it wasn't a great game, but occasionally, Cameron noticed his dad talking to Susanna and pointing at the play, presumably trying to help her understand the game. The game ended in a 2 all draw. As soon as the final whistle blew and the players had shaken hands, Gary went straight across to Susanna, and they walked to the changing room together.

As Cameron approached them, he asked, "Are you waiting for me, Susanna, or going back with dad?"

"Gary has invited me to go to his house for a meal, then he'll bring me here for the party, but I need to go back to yours to change. I'm not really dressed for a party at the moment. So, if that's alright, I'll come with you. Then when I've changed, will you take me to his house?" Cameron smiled. "Yes, no problem."

Gary butted in, "You come as well, Cameron. Ruth will be pleased to see you." So it was sorted.

When they arrived, it was Mrs Webster that opened the door. "Hello Cameron, it's nice to see you again, and this must be Susanna, who I've heard quite a lot about. It's nice to meet you, Susanna. Come in, both of you."

As before, Susanna was quiet at first, but as time went by, she obviously began to feel more comfortable and relaxed. She chatted with Mr and Mrs Webster about home and the big differences between the cities and her little village and admitted that she had found it all a little daunting. Finally, she said, "I think that I would have gone home if it wasn't for Cameron."

Ruth looked at him and grinned. "It's always the same with you, Cameron. You always come to the rescue!" Cameron looked a bit embarrassed.

"Don't tease him, Ruth. That's just Cameron being Cameron," her mum responded with a smile.

"Can we change the subject, please?" Cameron asked.

They all laughed. Eventually, Susanna produced a birthday card and passed it to Gary, along with a box wrapped in birthday paper. Gary looked a little surprised.

"Thank you." The card joined the rest on the window sill, and he opened the box to discover a half pint pewter tankard. Now he was really surprised but obviously genuinely pleased. "I hope you like it," she said.

"It's a nice surprise; yes, I do like it, and it will get well used."

As they walked through the door of the club, Matthew was first to spot them. Addressing Gary, he said, "I see you've already collared the best looking girl here," then noticing Ruth just behind, he continued, "That's best looking after you, of course, Ruth."

Chapter: 29

The early evening passed pleasantly with small talk amongst themselves until the DJ started the dance music. As usual, the girls, including Susanna, were the first onto the floor but then started to get the boys up. Cameron noticed Ruth whisper something to Susanna. At first, she seemed to hesitate and then walked over to Gary with her hand out. He didn't need a second invitation. Ruth went straight for Cameron. After that, Gary and Susanna were almost inseparable on the dance floor. Cameron was delighted that she was having a good time. At one point, when they were together, he said to Gary, "I hope that you are not leading her on. She is a bit naïve, but she obviously likes you."

Gary was quick to reply, "Honestly, Cameron, I'm not. I've never liked a girl in this way before. I think I'm beginning to know how you feel about Coral now."

As the evening drew to a close, the last dances were announced, and Gary and Susanna were on the floor again. This time they had their arms around each other, and as the music finished, he kissed her. There was a slight pause, and then she kissed him back. It took a while to say their goodnights, but as they were leaving, Gary said to Cameron, "I'll treat you to lunch tomorrow, but only if you bring

Susanna; I'll bring Ruth to keep you company." There were smiles all around, and the arrangements were made.

On the way back to the Mason's, Cameron said, "I don't have to ask if you've had a good time."

"No, Cameron, you don't. I've had a great time, and I'll let you into a little secret. Tonight is the first time that I've been kissed by a boy, and it's obviously the first time that I've kissed a boy."

He looked at her, "And how was it?" he asked.

She smiled, "Nice," was the reply, "very nice."

Lunch the next day went very well, and afterwards, they went for a stroll on the Downs. Gary and Susanna were slightly ahead, holding hands when Ruth, who was linking him, turned to Cameron and said, "I've never seen Gary like this before. I think that he really likes her."

"Oh, he does," Cameron replied. "Last night, he told me that now, he thinks he knows how I feel about Coral."

She looked at him, "Really."

"Really," Cameron replied.

Sadly it was time for Cameron to think about the journey back to Exeter. After a lingering kiss between Gary and Susanna and a hug between Cameron and Ruth, the goodbyes were said. Ruth and Susanna hugged each other. Gary and Cameron shook hands.

Gary said, "Look after her for me, Cameron."

Cameron nodded, "I will. Don't worry."

Susanna was quiet at first on the drive back. "Are you alright?" Cameron asked, "You're very quiet."

"I'm just thinking," she replied.

"About what?" he responded.

"The whole weekend, and Gary. I've already told you that I've never had a boyfriend before now, and I'm not sure what's going on. I'm a bit confused. All this holding hands and kissing. Does it usually happen so fast?"

Cameron laughed. "It's no good asking me. I've only ever had one girlfriend, and that's Coral. But if it helps, I've known Gary a long time, and he's been with a few girls before, but I've never seen him treat any of them like he's treating you. I think he really likes you." She looked across at him, "That's good because I think that you can tell that I like him."

"We all can," he replied. She smiled at that.

She was quiet for a while then, "Cameron. There's something I've noticed about you."

"Oh. What's that?"

"We've been out a lot together since we met, but I've never seen you drink alcohol."

"That's because I don't drink it. It's not religious or anything like that. I did try it once, and I didn't like it. So why drink something you don't like just to be one of the boys? It's never been an issue with my friends. They just accept it. Only once has it caused a problem."

"What happened?" she asked.

He told her about the incident after the cricket match. He continued, "It does have advantages, though. For instance, I know that I am fit to be driving us back to Exeter. Also, in the past, I've seen that it does make people do and say stupid things." He laughed, "If I say or do something stupid, I know that I can't blame the drink."

As they got closer to Exeter, he asked, "So do you think that you'll keep in touch with Gary." She nodded and smiled.

"He's given me his home telephone number. I've agreed to phone him next Friday when he will be back from Bath. It's easier for me to phone him because no one ever answers the phone in the halls. It's never for them, and they can't be bothered going looking for the person it's for. He's told me to reverse the charges."

After one of their lectures during the following week, she asked, "When do you think that you will be seeing Coral again?"

He sighed, "I'm not sure. Christmas would be nice, and we've thought about New Year in Edinburgh, but that's expensive, and most of the hotels are already booked, so I can't see us doing that. At the moment, I'm not sure when we'll get together."

She was quiet, and then she said, "I've been in Edinburgh for New Year. New Year's Eve is great, but most places are shut on New Year's Day. You'd love it, though!"

They went for lunch on the following Saturday. He could tell that she was in a very good mood. He guessed why. "How was your call with Gary last night?"

"Good, we talked for ages, and he's coming down next Friday. His dad is going to book them hotel rooms."

Cameron looked at her. "Them!"

"Oh! Yes. He's bringing Ruth so that we can all go out together."

Cameron laughed. "Now I wonder whose idea that was?"

Susanna suggested that the evening before they left for the Christmas break, they had an evening meal out. Cameron agreed, and she said that she would book it. "It's a thank you," she said.

"A thank you is not necessary," he said.

"I know, but I'd like to do it all the same."

He met her outside the halls, and they walked into town together. "Where are we going?" he asked.

She smiled, "Wait and see." When they were on Queen Street, she led him through the main entrance of a hotel.

He looked at her. "Are you sure? It will be expensive in here."

"Don't worry about that." They were approached by a waiter, and she told him that there was a table booked in the name of Butcher. He looked on a list, nodded and led them to a table on the far side of the dining room. Two people were already sitting there. They stood up as they approached, and their faces lit up.

"Cameron, this is my mum and dad. Mum, Dad, this is Cameron." Her mum gave her a big hug, whilst Mr Butcher shook his hand.

"Very pleased to meet you, Cameron," he said. "We've heard a lot about you, and it's all been good. You'll be pleased to know. Now let's all sit down."

The evening passed very pleasantly. Cameron was surprised by how much they knew about him. He hadn't realised how often Susanna had rung home, especially in the first few weeks. It was Mrs Butcher who said that they were sure that Susanna would have left the course if it wasn't for him. They were truly grateful. Cameron was a bit embarrassed but suggested that others may have done the same.

Susanna was quick to reply. "No, Cameron, I don't think that they would have been so supportive."

Mrs Butcher continued, "Now she seems to be thoroughly enjoying herself, and we are hearing a lot about someone called Gary."

Cameron laughed. "Gary is one of my best friends back in Bristol. Susanna and Gary go well together, believe me."

"We're going to find out for ourselves," smiled Mrs Butcher. "We've been ordered to invite him across for New Year." Cameron looked at Susanna. She was grinning.

"Does he know?" Cameron asked.

"No, but he will soon."

Mr Butcher spoke next. "Susanna tells us that you have a girlfriend." Cameron nodded.

"Coral and I have been together for ages, but we're finding it a bit of a struggle to see each other now. I'm down here, and she's in Edinburgh. I don't know when we'll get together again."

Mr Butcher took an envelope out of his pocket and handed it to Cameron.

"Maybe this will help," he said. "Go on, open it." Cameron did as he was told.

He sensed Susanna watching him as he opened the envelope. Inside was a confirmed booking for Mr C Mason and Miss C Browne for three nights over New Year in a hotel in Charlotte Square Edinburgh.

Mrs Butcher spoke, "It's all paid for, Cameron. Susanna's dad has business connections in Edinburgh. A few people owe him favours. We just called one in. Just one thing, if you can't make it, please ring and cancel the booking."

"Thank you," Cameron replied. "I don't know what else to say except thank you."

"One other thing," It was Mr Butcher this time. "It would be better if you went up by train. Parking in Edinburgh is a nightmare. This is our way of thanking you for looking after our daughter. We hope that you and Coral have a good time."

Chapter: 30

Coral put down the phone and almost skipped into the living room. "You look pleased. What's going on?" her mum asked. Coral could hardly contain herself.

"I've just been given the best Christmas present ever, but I'm not getting it until the New Year." Her parents looked puzzled, but as Coral explained her news, their expressions changed to ones of delight for their daughter. "I can't believe it," she kept saying, "Three whole days in Edinburgh with Cameron. I can't wait."

They took Mr Butcher's advice and went up by train. Coral could hardly stop smiling the whole way. When Cameron asked her what she was smiling at, she replied, "I can't believe it. We've got three whole days together and by ourselves. When we were in France and Ireland, we were never really on our own. Those holidays were lovely, but our parents were always there. Now it's just us!"

Having met Susanna's parents, Cameron knew that it would be a very good hotel, but it turned out to be much better than he expected. It was a very high-class establishment. After they had signed in, they were shown to their room, which turned out to be a beautifully decorated twin room with views over the square. It was Coral who

213

spoke first. "This is lovely, Cameron. I've never been in anywhere as posh as this."

"Neither have I," was his slightly muted response. She noticed that. "You were hoping for a double bed, weren't you?" He nodded.

She came close and put her arms around him. "I love you, Cameron, but this is right for us at the moment. We don't want to make any silly mistakes and ruin things at university. I'm not on the pill. Why would I be? I'm never going to sleep with anyone else except you, and you're down in Exeter, and I'm up here, so I don't need the pill. Let's just make the best of this time together. Kiss me – please." He did, and deep down, he knew that she was right.

After a meal in the hotel restaurant, they went for a walk along Princes Street. It was still early evening, and the souvenir shops were still open, and their lights spilt out onto the pavement as if beckoning them in. They browsed in a few of them but saved their money. They looked at the names that were on the Clan souvenirs. Cameron discovered that anyone with the surname 'Mason' might be associated with the Sinclair Clan. He was amused to find that there didn't seem to be a similar association for anyone named Browne. At this, Coral pulled a mock sulky face.

By now, it was time to head towards the north end of Princes Street to watch the torchlight parade that always happened on December 30th. Cameron noticed that every so often, Coral would squeeze his hand as if to reassure him that she did love him. People were starting to gather now, and they found a spot in the crowd and waited for the procession. He let go of her hand and put his arm around her shoulder, and pulled her close to him. She turned to look at him, and he whispered, "And I love her." She smiled and whispered back, "And I love him."

They heard the pipes and drums first, and then the torches appeared. There seemed to be hundreds of them bringing an orangey-yellow smoky glow to the night sky as they crossed North Bridge on their way to Princes Street. The procession filled the whole width of the street, and once it had passed, which seemed to take ages, along with the rest of the good-natured crowd, they started to follow it, eventually arriving at Holyrood Park. They mingled with the crowd for a while, checked out some of the stalls and then slowly strolled back up the Royal Mile towards the Castle, occasionally stopping to look in the shop windows.

Back in the hotel, they took it in turns to use the en suite. By the time Cameron came out, Coral was in bed. He bent over to kiss her, and then laughingly, she said, "You can get in for a cuddle, but no hanky panky."

He didn't need a second invitation. After a while, she said, "I love you, Cameron, but I think you should get in your own bed now. It's been nice, but if we are not careful, we might get carried away."

In the dark, they talked for a while, and then she said, "Do you remember that first evening in Ireland?"

"Yes. What about it?"

She continued, "You told me that I wasn't a game to you like it was for some of the other boys that you knew. Just now was the first time that you have really touched me, and Cameron, it was so nice."

Then she laughed. "I did notice that you liked it as well."

After breakfast, they went into town. Even though Coral had already been on a Tour Bus, she thought that Cameron would enjoy it. "It's the best and easiest way to see Edinburgh," she told him. They sat at the front on the top deck so that they could get a good view of everything. The driver gave a running commentary. As the bus turned one corner, they could see and hear someone playing the bagpipes. He wasn't much more than a teenager, and he was dressed in a traditional style costume, kilt, white shirt, jacket and Glengarry cap.

As they passed, the driver commented that "There's nothing like a good bagpipe player," he paused and then continued, "and he's nothing like a good bagpipe player." Cameron thought that was quite funny.

They got off at Holyrood Palace and wandered through the park. They thought about going inside the palace but decided against that, but they did look in the Palace Shop, and they both picked up a couple of souvenirs for their mums. Then it was back on the bus to complete the tour.

Afterwards, they decided that they needed something to eat, and halfway down Rose Street, they found a pleasant little café with a fairly extensive menu. Later they visited the art gallery. Some of the paintings were huge, and they both wondered how the artists managed to produce such wonderful paintings. Some were so detailed that they almost looked like photographs.

By now, it was time to head back to the hotel, and instead of going along Princes Street itself, they strolled through the gardens where preparations were well underway for the evening's festivities. Back at the hotel, the receptionist asked if they were going to book into the restaurant and had they enjoyed the day. "Yes to both," Coral replied.

Cameron read her name badge and asked, "Beth, have you any advice about the best way to enjoy tonight's celebrations?"

"Don't leave it too late to get onto Princes Street. It soon gets crowded." Then she screwed up her face. "If you are feeling energetic, some people like to run the whole length of the Royal Mile, but not me! There are usually several bands in the gardens. Just stroll until you find one that's to your liking. But where ever you are, you will be able to see the fireworks. Have a good time."

Just after 10.00 pm, they were back on Princes Street. Beth was right. It was already crowded. Groups of people were wandering up and down the street. It was obvious that some were already worse for wear, but it was all good-natured. Coral and Cameron, hand in hand, wandered through the gardens one way and then back along the street the other way. They had stopped a couple of times to listen to the groups, but it was the one that they had heard first that they went back to listen to.

As midnight approached, they could feel the excitement building, and then the countdown started, and everyone

218

joined in. At zero, there were huge cheers. People were hugging and kissing each other, even kissing complete strangers. Then fireworks started. Cameron put his arms around Coral and kissed her. "Happy New Year," he said, and he held her tight to him. She looked up at him with a huge smile on her face. "Happy New Year, Cameron. This is the best ever."

After the fireworks, they stayed on the street for a while longer, enjoying the atmosphere. Nearly everyone they passed wanted to wish them a Happy New Year, or shake their hands or even hug them. Then slowly, they made their way back to the hotel. Beth was still on duty.

"Did you have a good time?" She enquired.

It was Coral that answered. "It was lovely, thank you."

Beth continued, "You do know that most places, including most shops, will be closed tomorrow. A few souvenir shops might be open, and I think that the Castle is open, but not much else."

"We'll find something to do," said Cameron, and Beth wished them goodnight.

Chapter: 31

Back in Exeter, the first thing Susanna asked was, "Did you get to Edinburgh?" Before he had a chance to answer, she could tell by the smile on his face that they did.

"We did. Thanks to your parents and we had a lovely time together. It's the first time that we have spent so long together on our own. The only thing wrong was that it passed too quickly." He continued, "And how was your New Year?" But he already knew because he had seen Gary at the club before heading back to Exeter.

"It was lovely." She smiled. "We had a great time together, and after Gary had gone back home, mum told me that they thought he was charming, and they approved of the friendship, so that made it even better."

Gary had been full of it. "I got invited to Suffolk for New Year," he told Cameron. "It was a complete surprise."

"Did you accept?" Cameron asked. Gary looked at him. "What do you think? I wasn't going to turn down the chance to spend a few days with Susanna."

"How did it go?" Cameron asked.

"If you're asking did I get on with her parents, then I think it went well. I know that I enjoyed it, and Susanna and I managed to get a lot of time together."

Cameron smiled. "That's good then."

"You don't seem a bit surprised," Gary continued. "Did you know that I was going to get an invite?"

Cameron laughed. "I had an inkling that it was in the offing."

"You never said."

"Not my place to," Cameron replied.

Chapter: 32

Almost as soon as they met up again after the holiday, one of the first things Lorna asked Coral was, "How was your holiday?"

"It was good," Coral replied, "Very good," and she went on to tell her about New Year. When she had finished, Lorna gave her a big hug.

"I am so pleased for you; that should keep you both happy for a while."

Later in the week, it was Sean who asked if she had enjoyed the holiday. Her face lit up as she nodded and replied,

"I did, thank you, and New Year was lovely." Sean raised a quizzical eyebrow.

Before Coral could explain, Lorna butted in. "She spent New Year up here with Cameron, in one of those posh hotels in Charlotte Square."

"How did that come about?" he asked. Coral told the whole story. Sean seemed really pleased for her. "It's good to see you smiling so much, Coral. I'm happy for you. We all are."

"Thank you. We didn't think that we were going to get together at all, so it really was nice of Susanna's dad to sort it for us."

It was Craig who tried to spoil things. "Do you really trust him with Susanna?"

She looked daggers at him. "I don't really need to answer that," she almost growled at him. "I know that I am lucky because he's a good looking boy, and lots of girls have fancied him. I know that because they've told me, and much to their disappointment, he's never been tempted by any of them. I think that you've just spoilt my evening and our friendship Craig."

She stood up and turned to Lorna, "I'm leaving now, but you don't have to come with me."

Lorna jumped up. "I'll come," and she turned to Craig, "You idiot."

Outside, she linked Coral. "Are you alright?" Coral nodded.

"I'm fine. Why did he have to say that?"

"Don't worry about him. He's just jealous of Cameron. The others are obviously happy for you. They're probably giving him the rounds of the kitchen right now."

They hadn't gone far when Sean caught them up. "Coral, take no notice of Craig. We were all pleased for you. We could tell that you'd had a great time. I hope he hasn't spoilt things for me or the rest of us. Back there, right now, Craig is not the flavour of the month, and he's getting some stick."

They stopped walking. Coral turned to Sean. "I have no problem with you or the others, but it will be a long time before I speak to Craig again, except when I have to. He doesn't even know Cameron; if he did, he wouldn't have even let a thought like that enter his head."

Sean just nodded. Then he said, "Coral, please turn round and come back; it's still early. I'd have come after you anyway, but the others did ask me to try and persuade you to come back."

"I just want to go back to my room now, Sean. But thank you for coming after me. It was nice of you." She turned to Lorna, "You go back if you like. I don't mind."

Lorna shook her head. "I'll come with you, pet. I want to make sure that you are alright. Thanks, Sean. We'll see you all tomorrow."

Sean nodded. "Okay, and Coral, I'm with you on this."

Back at halls, they sat and talked about all sorts. Coral was suddenly surprised when Lorna said, "You obviously miss Cameron, but do you know what I miss?" Coral shook her head. Lorna continued, "Going to the match with my dad. We are Newcastle fans. When I was at home, we hardly missed a game."

Coral was a bit surprised. "You don't look like a football fan." Then she laughed, "But I don't know what I think a football fan should look like."

She paused. "I used to go and watch Cameron play football and cricket before they moved to Bristol."

Lorna was quick to respond. "So you understand football?" Coral nodded. Lorna went on, "I've been thinking about this for a while. I do miss the football, so how about we go and watch Hibs one Saturday?" It's not Newcastle, but it's better than nothing." Coral smiled, possibly for the first time in a couple of hours.

"Why not? It'll be a change."

The next day as they arrived for lectures, Coral and Lorna were surrounded by the group, all anxious to know if Coral was alright.

It was Alison who spoke first. "Coral, are you okay? We hoped that you would have come back. We sent Sean after you."

"I'm fine she replied, and Sean did his best, but the evening was spoilt for me. I just wanted to go back. Lorna looked after me."

Shelley spoke next. "I think Craig is regretting what he said. I'm afraid that we gave him a hard time after you left, and it wasn't long afterwards that he left. I think that he might try and make some kind of apology before long."

But he didn't. Not for a while anyway. It was several days before he stopped her as she was leaving the lab.

"Coral, I'm sorry about the other night. I didn't mean to upset you." "Apology accepted," she replied and tried to move past him.

"Is that all you're going to say?" he asked.

She nodded, "What else do you want me to say?"

He looked a bit downcast. "I don't know," he admitted. "I was hoping that you might forgive me."

"Maybe later, but at the moment, I can't do that. Now, if you don't mind, I need to catch Lorna up," and she left him standing at the door.

The incident had upset Coral, and she was desperate to speak to Cameron. On Friday evening, she rang Bristol in the hope that Cameron was home to play football on Saturday. Luckily, she caught him just as he had arrived home. She told him all about the incident with Craig. He could tell that she was upset.

"Coral, I love you. I'm not interested in anyone else. There's never been anyone else. If it makes you feel better, I can tell you that Susanna and Gary are definitely together now. She can tell you herself if you like. She's here now, and I'm just about to go and take her round to see Gary. They are off to a show together at The Colston Hall."

Deep down, she knew that she had nothing to fear from Susanna or any other girl for that matter, but it was nice to chat with him, and the phone call was quite a long one. In the end, Cameron had to end it because Susanna was due at the Webster's.

When she got back to her room, Lorna was waiting for her.

"Well, she asked, how did that go? It lasted long enough."

Coral smiled. "It was good, I knew really, but I just wanted to talk to him. I do miss him."

A week later, on Friday, when they were all together at lunchtime, Alison laughingly asked if anyone was doing anything exciting at the weekend.

Lorna responded. "Coral and I are going to watch the Hibs."

There was a short pause before Sean asked, "Really?"

Lorna and Coral both spoke at the same time. "Really," they said. Then Lorna went on to explain how she was missing the football and Coral had used to watch Cameron play, so they thought that it would be an interesting change.

Sean seemed to be thinking. "Don't Hibs play in green?" Lorna nodded. Sean continued, "The Rovers, that's Shamrock Rovers back home, play in green as well. I used to go and watch them sometimes. It's been a while since I went to a game. Can I come with you?"

Lorna looked at Coral. "Why not," Coral replied. Then a few others started to take an interest, and in the end, there were six of them planning to go to the game.

In truth, it wasn't a very good game. Neither side played very well, and to make matters worse, Hibs lost one-nil to St Johnstone. Lorna remarked that she hadn't expected Hibs to be as good as Newcastle, but she thought that they might have played a bit better than they did. Shelley and Alison weren't really bothered about the game at all or the result, but they did admit that one or two of the players were quite dishy, much to everyone's amusement. Sean thought that the best bit of the afternoon was the bag of chips that he had bought after the game.

Lorna and Coral decided that they would head back to the halls and catch up on some work. They got together in Lorna's room, and when they had finished the work, they sat around chatting.

Lorna surprised Coral when she said, "Next time that I go home for the weekend, would you like to come?"

"That would be nice, but are you sure?" Coral replied.

Lorna nodded. "I wouldn't have asked if I didn't mean it." She smiled, "and I might even take you to watch a proper football team!"

One Wednesday evening, a week or so later, Lorna said, "I'm going home at the weekend. Do you want to come?"

Coral thought about it for a few seconds, then nodded, "Yes, please, but are you sure that it will be alright? Your parents won't mind?" Lorna laughed, "It'll be fine, pet. I've already been in touch to check."

Chapter: 33

After lectures finished on Friday, they were on the platform at Waverley Station. It takes about an hour and a half to Newcastle, Lorna told her, and it goes through some lovely countryside. If the weather is good, you'll enjoy the landscape. Sure enough, Coral did enjoy the journey, and she was looking forward to the change of scenery. At one point during the journey, in the distance, Lorna pointed out Lindisfarne.

"It's lovely on the island," she said. "I'll take you there one day."

When they arrived in Newcastle, they caught the Metro from Monument and, not long afterwards, arrived in Tynemouth. A short walk later, Lorna turned into the drive of a modern detached house. "Here we are," she said. She opened the door, "Mum," she shouted, "We're here."

Mrs Moore appeared from the kitchen. She gave Lorna a hug and then turned to Coral. "You must be Coral. It's nice to meet you, pet. Drop your bags there, and I'll make a brew. Lorna can show you your room later." They passed a pleasant half-hour chatting about life in Edinburgh and Coral's life back home. "I've also been told that you've got a boyfriend."

Coral's face lit up. "He's called Cameron: We've been together almost as long as I can remember. But it's hard at the moment. I'm up in Edinburgh, and he's down in Exeter." Mrs Moore shook her head and smiled. "Well, pet, between the two of you, you didn't manage that very well, did you? But I wish you luck."

After the evening meal, Mr Moore turned to Coral. "I've heard that you quite like football."

"That's right. I used to go and watch Cameron when he lived near me. He was a good player. No! That's not right. He still is a good player. Every so often, he manages to get back to Bristol to play for Clifton Athletic. He really enjoys playing."

Mr Moore continued, "And does he support any team?"

"He used to go and watch City sometimes before they moved to Bristol, but I don't think that he's ever been to watch either of the Bristol teams since he's lived down there."

Mr Moore smiled, "And what about you; do you support a team?"

She shook her head, "No, not really, but Dad watches City, so I do look for their results sometimes, but they are not doing very well at the moment."

He laughed, "No, they're not. Well tomorrow, if you like, we'll take you to watch the Magpies. How does that sound?"

Before she could answer, Mrs Moore piped up, "Coral. Don't feel under pressure to go. I'll happily take you shopping in the city if you prefer."

Coral smiled. "I'll go to the football. I'd already guessed that we might be going. A few weeks back, after we went to watch Hibs, Lorna said that she'd take me to watch a decent team."

"That's settled then. Football it is. Oh, by the way," he turned to Lorna, "I've got a surprise for you. We're going corporate; we've got three tickets in the firm's box. There were three going spare, so I said that I'd take them." He turned to Coral. "With a box, you can sit outside or inside, which is great if it's cold, but if you sit outside, you still get the atmosphere and hear the crowd."

"You get yummy food as well," Lorna added.

The metro back into Newcastle was quite crowded, and although the three of them got seats, they weren't together. Coral found herself sitting next to an elderly gentleman who chatted away pleasantly all the way into Newcastle.

When they got off, Lorna had a big smile on her face. "Well, what was the old man telling you?"

Coral shook her head and laughed, "I hardly understood a word he was saying; I just kept nodding and saying what I thought he wanted me to say. Most of the time, I think that he was telling me about football. He didn't seem to take offence, and I must have got some of it right because he kept calling me pet."

Mr Moore laughed, "Everyone calls everyone pet round here. You'll get used to it. Now stay close as we walk to the ground. It's already getting busy."

Lorna linked her. "I'll look after you."

The closer they got to St James's Park, Coral could feel the atmosphere building up, and she began to feel quite excited. Even back home, she'd never been to watch either of the Manchester teams and already she could tell that this crowd was going to be much bigger than the crowd at the Hibs match.

Mr Moore showed the three tickets to the steward at the corporate entrance, and he waved them through. They took the lift to the level where the box was. Another steward checked the tickets again, and they were shown into the box. Coral hadn't really known what to expect, and she was quite surprised. The seats facing the pitch looked surprisingly comfortable, and sliding doors allowed access to the seats outside. At the back of the box, on a table, tea and coffee were available, as well as warm food, and in the corner, there was a small bar. Help yourself to anything you like, she was told. Lorna was right; the food looked 'yummy'.

As kick-off approached, Lorna said, "I'm going to sit outside, but you can stay in if you want to."

"I'll sit with you," Coral replied. The game didn't start too well for Newcastle, and much to the home fans frustration, it wasn't too long before Crystal Palace were 2 goals up.

Lorna turned to Coral, "This isn't supposed to happen. We were expected to win this today, but while we've got Shearer on the pitch, we are always likely to get a goal back."

She was right, but it wasn't until deep in the second half that Alan Shearer scored a goal. Coral had never heard a noise like it as the crowd behind the goal celebrated wildly.

"That's the Gallowgate End," Lorna told her. However, no matter how hard they tried, Newcastle couldn't manage an equaliser.

When the game was over, Mr Moore turned to Coral, smiled and said, "Well, I'm not bringing you again if that's the effect you have on the team."

Coral laughed, "Oh, it's my fault, is it?"

He nodded. "Football fans are very superstitious and like to keep to the same routine before every game. You're the only difference to our routine today, but we'll let you off. Anyway, have you enjoyed it?" She nodded, "Yes and thank you for bringing me, and I'm sorry that I brought bad luck."

He laughed. "It's how football goes sometimes. That's why we love it."

Chapter: 34

Coral's worst fears were starting to come true. It was difficult to keep in touch. Neither of them had direct access to a phone. No one would answer the phone in the halls unless they were sure that it was for them. If someone did answer a ringing phone expecting it to be for them, and it wasn't, they were usually reluctant to go and seek out the student it was for. There were two reasons for this; the intended recipient might not be around, and it would delay the call for the person who was expecting it.

Often they would wait for twenty seconds or so and then tell the caller that they couldn't find the person they wanted without having made too much effort to find them at all. Coral and Cameron did write, but they both admitted that they weren't very good at letter writing and often there was not too much to tell, and the letters became fewer and fewer.

When the summer break arrived, Coral went back to the surgery and asked if there was still a chance that she could help out. Hannah was delighted to see her and quizzed her about life in Edinburgh and how the course was going. Coral explained that the Saturday mornings had been very useful, and one of the tutors had complimented her on her initiative. The Saturday experience had turned out to be very useful on a number of occasions. Hannah was pleased to hear it. Now that Coral was officially a student, Hannah offered her extra hours, and so it was agreed that Coral could attend the surgery for two days a week, perhaps Tuesdays and Wednesdays, but it had to be regular. No ringing up and cancelling at the last minute.

The downside to this arrangement meant that she would probably not get to spend much time with Cameron unless he came up to visit. When she explained it all to Cameron, he understood the situation completely. From his point of view, the cricket team was doing well, so he didn't want to miss too many matches. He said that he was coming up to see Uncle Ben for a few days, so they could get together during that visit.

He came up one Thursday in the middle of August, and instead of staying at the Browne's, he collected Coral, and they went and stayed for a few nights with Uncle Ben.

Chapter: 35

Not many weeks after the start of the second year at university, there was another upheaval for the Mason's. Mr Mason was offered a twelve-month secondment to the company's site at Toulouse in France. The offer included a substantial 'one off' financial inducement that was too good to turn down. Mrs Mason was reluctant to go with him, but Cameron insisted she went.

"You can't turn down the chance of living in France for a year; the weather will be great for a start," he said.

However, his mum was worried about him, and "What about the house?" she wondered. There were long family discussions where every conceivable possibility was considered. However, in the end, she agreed that it was too good an opportunity to pass up. After all, it was only for a year, and so finally she agreed to go. They decided to keep the house so that Cameron would have somewhere to come back to at weekends and between terms. "No big parties trashing the place, though," his dad warned him.

On the first few occasions, when he was back in Bristol for the weekend, he didn't always have the house to himself because Susanna came with him. However, as time went by, she started to get invitations to stay at the Webster's, and that did mean that he had the house to himself, and he quite enjoyed that.

With Christmas arriving, Cameron had a dilemma. Where was he going to spend it? Christmas in France would be a new experience, or should he stay in Bristol? More importantly, were he and Coral going to get together?

On the last day of the autumn term, he said his goodbyes to Susanna and drove back to Bristol. He'd only been back at the house for a couple of hours when the phone rang. It was Mrs Browne. She was a bit surprised when he answered and even more surprised when he explained that his parents were in France.

"Coral never told us about this," she said. Cameron admitted that he'd never told Coral, mainly because they'd hardly been in touch with each other over the last few months. She sounded worried, "You haven't fallen out with each other, have you?" She asked.

"No, Mrs Browne, we haven't. It's just difficult to get to speak to each other, and we both know that we are not very good at writing letters."

"Well, I really rang to ask your mum if they had plans for Christmas, but now I suppose that you'll be off to spend Christmas in France."

"I think Mum and Dad have decided to stay in France, but I haven't decided what I'm doing yet. I might stay here. I've got work to do."

"But what about Christmas Day and Boxing Day, she asked. "You can't spend it on your own. Why don't you come up here? I thought that your parents might be visiting your uncle, so I was going to suggest that we all meet up on one of the days," she paused. "Well, Cameron, what do you say?"

"Mrs Browne, if you could see me, you'd see that I am grinning from ear to ear. Of course, I'd love to come. Thank you."

She laughed. "That's settled then, Cameron. I know someone who will be very happy when we tell her. She's not home yet. Her dad's going to meet her at Piccadilly tomorrow night. They finish today. You can come up whenever it suits you. Just give me a ring to tell me when you are coming up."

"I will, and thank you, Mrs Browne, Goodbye."

Mr Browne met Coral at the station the following evening. He noticed that she seemed a bit subdued.

"Are you alright?" He asked, "You're very quiet; it's not like you." She just nodded.

"I was just thinking about Cameron. I haven't seen him in ages or spoken to him, and I do miss him."

Her dad smiled. "Do you want the good news or the bad news?"

"I'll have the bad news first," she replied.

"The bad news then. Mr and Mrs Mason have moved to France for a year. Mr Mason got transferred there, back in the autumn, so they are going to be in France for Christmas."

All sorts of thoughts went through Coral's mind, the worst one being that Cameron would probably go to France for Christmas.

"What's the good news then?" she sighed. He turned to look at her. "You'll like this," he said, "Cameron is coming to us for Christmas."

"Dad! This is the best news ever. You're not kidding me, are you?" "How did this happen?"

"No love, it's true," and he went on to explain the phone call.

Cameron decided to go up the day before Christmas Eve. He rang up a day or two before. It was Coral who answered the phone. She tried to persuade him to come up even sooner.

"Mum says that you can come up tomorrow if you want." However, much as he would have liked to, he resisted the temptation. "I've got work to do", he told her, "and I want to finish it. I don't want to be having to rush it in the last few days before I go back to Exeter". She was disappointed, but she understood.

They both enjoyed Christmas. There was a lot of catching up to do. They hadn't seen each other since the few days they had spent with Uncle Ben. As soon as they were together, though, it was as if they had never been apart.

Chapter: 36

As part of the course, the students sometimes went to Edinburgh Zoo to see the resident vets in action. Lorna and Coral both enjoyed these occasions. During one of these visits, when talking to Donald, one of the vets, Coral admitted that she would love to work in a zoo or safari park when she was qualified. He asked if she was serious. She nodded.

"Well," he continued, "During the summer, it gets quite busy, and we sometimes take on students to help out. Would you be interested?" Lorna and Coral looked at each other and then, almost in unison, said, "Yes."

"I'll take your details then, and if we decide that we need extra hands, we'll be in touch."

He was as good as his word, and a few weeks later, the tutor kept Lorna and Coral back after some lab work. We've got a message for you both from Donald at the zoo, she told them. They're offering you both a placement for the summer, but it's not at the zoo. It's at the Highland Wildlife Park. Remember, it's voluntary, so no pay, but you will get board and lodgings. It's quite remote up there, so you might want to think about it. Give me an answer by the end of the week.

It took a good deal of discussion before they made their decision. On the plus side, it was a great opportunity to further their careers, and it was a wonderful chance to work with animals that were not the kind that you would get at a normal surgery. The downside was the remoteness, and that meant, as far as Coral was concerned, there was very little chance of seeing Cameron over the summer. Lorna knew that this was presenting Coral with a real dilemma. Coral and Cameron had hardly seen each other during the past year as it was. Taking this placement would most probably mean that they wouldn't get together at all over the summer. In the end, Lorna said, "If Cameron was here now, what would he tell you to do?" When Lorna put it like that, Coral didn't even have to think.

"He'd tell me to do it," she said. That settled it.

The next weekend, when she hoped that he would be back at the house in Bristol, she phoned him and explained what had gone on. She could tell that he was disappointed, but just as she'd known that he would, he told her that she had done the right thing.

"We'll have plenty of time together in the future. It will all be worth it in the end," he said.

Lorna and Coral spent most of the summer at the Highland Wildlife Park. The tutor was right. It was remote, but they both had a wonderful time. The placement was so successful that they were invited back for the following year. However, for Coral, the downside was that she never got to see or hear from Cameron at all. Back at home, for a few days, she was full of it, and her parents could tell that she had enjoyed the whole experience and they were both really happy for her. But then, all too soon for Mrs Browne's liking, she was off back to Scotland for the start of her third year.

Not long after the start of Cameron's final year, his parents returned from France. However, Uncle Ben had been in touch with Mr Mason with a very attractive proposition. He wanted him to work with him on a new project, but it would involve them returning to the north. In addition, he was finding the big house was getting a little too much for him now; so he had a suggestion. He would have an annexe built, attached to the main house, which he would move into, and they could move into the main house.

There was only one problem. If they sold the house, what was going to happen to Cameron at the weekends when he came back to play football? It was Matthew who provided the solution. He had his own rather superior two-bedroom apartment now, which was close to the city centre. One Saturday evening at the club, when the group were all together, Cameron mentioned the dilemma.

"That's not a problem, Cameron. I've got plenty of room; you can stay with me whenever you like. You can even leave stuff in the bedroom if you want." Once his parents heard that, the decision was made. The house went on the market, and just after Christmas, his parents moved back north.

The rest of his final year was pretty hectic and was over before he knew it. Later, when he looked back, it was during this time that he realised that he had completely lost touch with Coral.

In Edinburgh, Coral suddenly realised that she had not heard from Cameron in ages. She wasn't sure how it had happened, and she knew that it wasn't a deliberate act by either of them. Her third year had been the hardest so far, and work seemed to be taking over her life. Fortunately, she and Lorna still got on extremely well and were virtually inseparable.

One weekend towards the end of the term, she decided to try and ring him in Bristol. Even if he wasn't at home, she could speak to his mum or dad, and they could at least let him know that she had called. She was very surprised, therefore, when there was a recorded message telling her that the number she had called was unobtainable. She checked that she had dialled the correct number and then redialled. Once again, she got the same result. This left her confused and a little worried. She got in touch with her mum and asked her to try the Mason's number, but the result was just the same.

The only conclusion that they could come to was that the Masons had moved, but Mrs Browne felt sure that if that had happened, Mrs Mason would have let her know where they had moved to. Coral was a little worried, but she trusted that Cameron would eventually get in touch. After all, when he first moved to Bristol, he had promised that no matter what, he would come back for her. She believed him then, and she still believed him.

Chapter: 37

Cameron was not having much success with his job applications. He joined a job agency, and in addition, he had applied to a host of companies who he thought might need a chemistry graduate, even though they hadn't been advertising vacancies. Very few bothered to reply, and those that did often referred to the current climate and informed him that, unfortunately, they weren't hiring at the present time.

Matthew could see that he was getting a bit low, so one evening, he suggested accompanying him on one of his school assignments. "It's got to be better than kicking your heels around in the flat," he told him.

Two days later, Cameron found himself visiting a little country school on the edge of the Cotswolds. They went and introduced themselves at the school office and then unloaded the photographic gear from the car and set it up in the school hall. Matthew was booked to take class photos, team photos and photos of each individual child. Cameron was surprised at the amount of equipment that Matthew used. There were two Nikon cameras for a start. "One is a back-up," Matthew told him; several lenses and studio lighting, with all the accessories, and rolls and rolls of film.

As the day progressed, Cameron became more and more interested. He watched as Matthew adjusted the lighting, changed the lenses and chatted with children. Matthew admitted later that he really enjoyed this interaction with the children.

The class and team photos needed careful arrangement, usually with the children in two or three rows, perhaps with one row sitting on the floor, one row sitting on a school PE bench and one row standing behind with the tallest of the children in the middle of the back row. When it came to the individual photos, he noticed how Matthew got them to sit with a shoulder slightly towards the camera and with a very gentle tilt of the head. Most importantly, he realised that Matthew always chatted to each child and usually managed to raise a smile and at that moment, the flash fired. He also noticed that he took more than one of each child. "There's nothing worse than a portrait of a child with their eyes closed," Matthew told him later. "Mum and Dad will not buy it, so take two or three to be on the safe side."

Cameron's job was to stick a label on each film canister. These were pre-printed by the company. The name of the school was on the label. All Cameron had to do was number them and then fill in the schedule with brief details about what was on each roll.

Back at the flat, Cameron started asking questions about the cameras and especially the different lenses and the lighting setups that Matthew had used. Matthew could see that Cameron was really interested, and they spent a long time going through the photography basics. Cameron was surprised to learn that Matthew never saw the results of his work.

He just sent the rolls of film off to the company, and they did the rest. They developed, printed and mounted the photos and then had them delivered back to the school.

"They must be alright," Matthew laughed, "because they keep sending me out to schools. The schools and parents must be satisfied. If you have enjoyed the day, why not come out with me again? I've nothing tomorrow, but on Thursday, it's a big job; a much bigger school than today."

Cameron thought about it, and the idea appealed to him. "Okay. I will. Are you busy tomorrow? I might go and buy a camera, and I could probably use some advice." Matthew agreed to go with him the next day. "However, don't go spending a lot of money," he told him. "The world of photography is changing. It won't be too long before cameras like mine will be obsolete and replaced with digital cameras. Roll film will become a thing of the past."

The next day, he bought a camera, and then they wandered around the city, and Matthew gave him a master class pointing out how the light worked; how to frame shots; how to have a main point of interest; how to keep things simple and not include too much. Cameron really enjoyed himself. He soon ran off a couple of rolls of film and put them in at the local Jessops store to get them developed. They offered a one-hour printing service, so he didn't have to wait long for the results. When they got back to the flat and examined the prints, Matthew was quite impressed. There were a few duds, but there were a lot that they both really liked.

"This is typical of you," Matthew remarked, "There doesn't seem to be anything that you can't do well. You'll be having my job before long."

Cameron laughed, "I doubt it."

"No, I mean it." Matthew picked out two or three pictures from the sets. "Look at these. Let's get them enlarged in black and white, mount and frame them and then take them to Henry in the art shop." Cameron looked at him. "Who's Henry?"

"He runs the art shop in the city, and he has a little gallery at the back of the shop. I put a lot of my work in there, and

252

he sells it for a small commission. These will soon sell, believe me."

"Where will I get them enlarged and printed, Jessops?"

Matthew shook his head. "No. I'll get them done at the professional lab where I take mine."

Matthew was true to his word. When the pictures came back, Cameron was delighted. They looked stunning. Then one evening, Matthew showed Cameron how to mount the pictures. "If you make the mounts a standard size, you can buy frames off the shelf. You don't need to spend more money getting them framed," he told him.

The following Saturday, they visited Henry's art shop, and Matthew introduced Henry to Cameron. When he saw the images, he whistled. "These will soon sell," he said. They watched as he hung them, and then all three went back to the front of the shop.

"How much do you think that they will sell for?" Cameron asked.

"How about I put £40 on them, and I'll take 10%?"

Matthew answered for him. "That'll be great, Henry. Thanks." They went for some lunch.

Cameron was sceptical. "No one will pay that," he said.

"Just you wait," Matthew replied.

Back at the flat, they were just getting ready to go to the club when the phone rang. Matthew answered it. "Cam, it's for you," and he held the phone out for him. Matthew watched with a smile on his face.

A voice at the other end said, "Hi Cameron. It's Henry. I've sold two of your pictures already, and you'll have to get one of them reprinted because I had two people fighting over it, so I've promised to get another copy for them."

Cameron was shocked. "I can't believe that, but thank you."

"No problem, Cameron. Just drop it in when it's done." Cameron turned to face Matthew.

"Told you," was all Matthew said.

At the club, Matthew was full of Cameron's success. "We've got a new David Bailey amongst us. If I'm not careful, he'll be taking over my job," he told them. Cameron shook his head and laughed.

"I don't think so. It's just beginner's luck."

Nevertheless, he was pleased with himself. An idea began to form in his mind. "I might as well get out and take a few photos", he thought. "Maybe I can sell a few more. It's something to do until a proper job comes along. I might make a few bob along the way." At the end of the evening, as they were all saying goodnight, Ruth asked him what his plans were for tomorrow.

"Why, have you got something in mind?" he asked.

"Not really," she replied, "But I was going to suggest that we should drive to some of the Cotswold villages, and you could try out this new camera of yours. You might take some more masterpieces. I'll drive if you like."

Cameron thought about it. "Okay, it sounds good."

They had a great day. Cameron had not really visited the Cotswolds before and didn't realise how attractive some of the villages were. Many of the villages had gift shops, and amongst the items for sale, there were usually paintings or sketches of the area. Cameron studied them. If he was going to take photos, he didn't want to reproduce the same as everyone else, and he said as much to Ruth, so they spent time trying to find something a bit different to photograph in each village. Ruth seemed to enjoy the challenge, and it turned out that she was rather good at finding views that he might have missed. When they had grown tired of looking for things to photograph, they looked for somewhere to have a snack, and on the way home, they found a nice village pub, so they stopped for dinner. She dropped him back at the flat.

"I've had a lovely day," she told him.

"Me too. Thank you. I'll get these printed tomorrow, and then we'll see what rubbish I've taken," and he laughed.

"They won't be rubbish, Cameron. Believe me."

She was right. When Matthew looked at them the following day, he was impressed. "Cameron, you've got the eye. They're not all great, but there are some very good ones. Let's get them printed up, mounted and framed and then down to Henry's, and don't forget Henry needs that reprint of the one he's already sold."

Later in the week, the prints were dropped off at Henry's. Henry handed over the £72 pounds that he'd already taken for the sold prints. He looked at the new ones.

"These are a bit different. They are not the run of the mill Cotswold pictures. I think that these will soon be gone." Again, he was right. They got a phone call just after closing time on Friday. "Hi, Cameron. I've got the £36 for the reprint, and I've sold five of the seven Cotswold prints that you left, so I have a further £180 for you to collect sometime."

Chapter: 38

Cameron collected the money the following day and bought a small pair of earrings for Ruth as a thank you token. He gave them to her that evening at the club.

"Cameron, they're lovely. You needn't have done, but thank you. Can I give you a kiss?"

He smiled, "Just this once," he replied.

During the evening, Matthew came and sat with him. "I've got a suggestion to put to you," he said.

"Go on, tell me."

"You might think that I'm stupid, but I think that you should pursue this photography lark quite seriously. Why not take a short course at the college. They last for about ten weeks. I've checked, there's one starting next Monday afternoon. It costs £30. You get instruction, use of the darkroom, and there are several studio setups you can use. If you get offered a chemistry job by an agency, you can always drop out of the photography course. You've nothing to lose, and it will help fill your time."

There was a pause. "Well, what do you think?" Matthew asked. "You've really thought about this, haven't you?" Cameron replied. Matthew nodded.

"I might as well try it then. I'll learn something if nothing else."

He enrolled on the course and thoroughly enjoyed himself. The lecturer was called Sarah, and she made everything sound simple. As well as the instruction, they were given assignments to complete for the next week. Cameron discovered the thrill of seeing his images gradually appear in the developer before being washed and put in the fixer. However, the thing that he liked best was using the studios. His school visits with Matthew proved invaluable as he had already learnt a few lighting setups, but he learnt several more, some of which gave very dramatic effects. His time with Matthew also proved useful when working with the models. He had learnt, from watching Matthew, how to pose the models, how to chat to them, how to put them at ease and get the best out of them. Sarah was impressed. "You're a natural in the studio, Cameron. You've done this before, I think." He explained about his school visits with Matthew. "Well, it shows," she said.

At the end of the ninth week, Megan, one of the models, caught up with Cameron on the way out. "Can I ask you something, Cameron?" "Sure," he replied.

"I really like some of the photos that you've done of me. Can I have some copies, and will you take some more of me?"

"You can certainly have some copies, but I haven't got access to a studio to do any studio work," he replied.

She smiled. "I've checked with Sarah. I can hire the studio by the hour. So will you do it?"

On Wednesday, they were back in the studio. Megan had brought several changes of clothes, and Sarah occasionally popped in to offer advice. Cameron tried all sorts of different poses with her and had borrowed a couple of lenses from Matthew so that he could get close up headshots and full-length shots as well as the standard head and shoulders shots. If Cameron was good in the studio with lighting effects, Megan was equally as good at posing. She was a natural. The two hours passed quickly. As they were packing to leave, Megan said, "Can I buy you a coffee as a thank you?"

Cameron shook his head. "I've really enjoyed this afternoon. I'll buy the coffee. You've paid for the studio."

On the way home, he decided to get the films developed and printed at the professional lab that Matthew used.

When the five rolls of film came back, Cameron was delighted. Matthew was impressed. "There are a few that are no good because she's got her eyes closed, but that happens, but most of them are good, and there are a few that are really good. She should be delighted with them. If I were you, I would only show the best. Let's get these three printed, mounted and framed."

Chapter: 39

On the following Monday, he was surprised to find that Megan was waiting for him at the college entrance. "Have you had the photos developed yet?"

He nodded, "But I haven't got them with me." He could see that she was disappointed. "I'll bring them round to yours, tomorrow or Wednesday."

He took the photos round to Megan's on Wednesday afternoon. When he arrived at the address that she had given him, he was impressed by the size of the property. It was huge, not quite so big as Uncle Ben's, but not so far off. There were several cars already on the driveway, but there was still plenty of room for his little Corsa. There were steps leading up to the front door. He rang the bell and was relieved when Megan herself opened the door. Her face lit up when she saw him standing there.

"Cameron!" Then she spotted the parcel under his arm. "Have you got some pictures for me?" He nodded.

"Come in. I can't wait to see them." She showed him into a room at the front of the house, and they sat down. He handed her the thirty or so small prints that he and Matthew had selected. He watched her face as she inspected them one by one, her expression slowly changing as each new photo appeared. Then she looked up at him. "These are great, Cameron. I just love them."

He reached down for the parcel that he had leant against the side of his chair and handed it to her. Inside were the three enlarged mounted and framed images that he and Matthew thought were the best.

"I like these the best," he said. She unwrapped them and placed them side by side on the floor. Her face lit up again.

"Cameron, they're wonderful. Can I keep them?"

He nodded. "I got them done especially for you."

She stood up. "I'm just going to get my mum." Not more than twenty seconds later, she returned with her mother. He stood up as they entered the room. Even if he hadn't been told, he would have known that this was her mother. Apart from the age difference, they were almost identical.

Megan introduced them and then said, "Look at these, Mum. Aren't they great? And there are all these little ones as well."

There was a pause whilst Mrs Chambers examined the large photos carefully. She turned to Cameron. "These are the best photos I've ever seen of Megan. I'll buy all three off you."

Cameron shook his head. "No, they're a gift for Megan. We had a great time in the studio, which she paid for, and I learnt a lot, so I think that's the least I could do."

"Are you sure?"

"Quite sure," he replied.

Megan interrupted, "Would you like a drink, Cameron? We were just going to make one when you arrived."

"Tea would be nice if it's not too much trouble." Megan disappeared and left her mother and Cameron together.

When Megan returned, she was carrying a tea tray with three mugs, teapot milk sugar and biscuits. The three of them spent a pleasant quarter of an hour chatting before Mrs Chambers stood up.

"I'll leave you two together. It's been very nice to meet you, Cameron. I had heard a bit about you. I'm sure that we'll meet again."

Cameron stood up. "It's been nice to meet you too," he replied, and he offered his hand for her to shake, which she did. Cameron and Megan sat talking for a while, and then he said that he thought that it was time to leave.

"Can we do some more photos together? Maybe we could do some outside this time?" she asked.

"Why not," he replied, and they agreed that they would arrange something the following week.

Later, when he was back at the flat, he realised that he had been politely interrogated by Megan's mum. He'd told her about the university, the lack of jobs, the visits to school with Matthew and his relative success in selling pictures at Henry's gallery. Finally, he told her about the college course and how much he had enjoyed it. When he had finished, she told him that she thought he had a talent for it and he should keep it up.

All this photography had really got him thinking. He was really enjoying himself, and everyone seemed to think that he was quite good at it. He had made a little money out of it thanks to the help from Matthew and Henry, but he wondered if it was possible to make a living from it. He knew that some of the portraits he had taken were more than just good. He could tell that by the reaction of the models at the college and Megan's mum in particular. On the final day of the course, Sarah had told him that he should visit the art gallery and look at the portrait paintings there. Not just look but study them carefully. "See if you can work out what makes them so good," she said.

He took her advice and spent a couple of afternoons at the gallery, looking at all the paintings, but especially the portraits. He soon realised what Sarah had meant. The ones he liked best all had similarities. It may have been the pose, the tilt of the head, the catch light in the eyes, or the fact that the subject appeared to be looking at the artist. The backgrounds were important as well; many of them had a real connection to the subject. He made a mental note to make sure that at least some of these things were included in his portraits.

He mentioned to Matthew that Megan wanted some photos taken outside. "Lighting and backgrounds can be tricky outside," Matthew told him, and so he offered to go with him, providing that he wasn't booked for a school shoot.

Chapter: 40

A few days later, they were on the Clifton Downs. Matthew had brought some portable lighting, and with his help, Cameron thought that he probably had some great images. He was aiming to get some fashion type shots, such as those he had seen in the magazines of the Sunday Papers. Matthew admitted that he had not done too much of this type of photography recently and had brought his camera as well. Just as she had been in the studio, Megan proved to be a natural model. She'd brought several costume changes. She managed to make the changes behind some handy bushes away from prying eyes.

Matthew was impressed. "She's good," he told Cameron.

Before they knew it, the afternoon was over. Matthew took the rolls of film straight to the lab that he used. "These need doing professionally," he told them. Meanwhile, Cameron took Megan home, and she invited him in. Almost as soon as they were inside, Megan's mum appeared.

"How did it go?" she asked.

"We'll have to wait and see," Megan replied. "But I had a great time. Cameron and Matthew were perfect gentlemen."

"I should hope so," her mother responded with a smile.

She turned to Cameron, "Correct me if I'm wrong, but weren't you a bit of a hero a few years back? You rescued a toddler from drowning in the lake in the park. It was you, wasn't it?"

Cameron nodded. "But it wasn't just me. Ruth and I did it between us. How did you know about that? It was a long time ago."

She smiled. "It's a long story Cameron, but basically, the daughter of one of our neighbours was the reporter who covered the story. She saw you leaving the last time you were here, and she remembered you. I bumped into her today. She told me quite a lot about the incident, and what you've just said about Ruth helping backs up what she said about you."

At this point, Megan interrupted. "What did she say, Mum?"

"She said that Cameron doesn't like the limelight."

Megan spoke again. "I don't remember reading any of this, Cameron. Tell us what happened." Reluctantly, Cameron told the story. When he had finished, he said, "It was nothing really. Anyone else would have done the same."

"Ah! But would anyone else there have known how to do mouth to mouth?" Mrs Chambers asked. "I doubt it," she continued.

Cameron shrugged his shoulders. "This is getting embarrassing. Can we change the subject?"

"See," said Mrs Chambers with a laugh. "You don't like the limelight." She went on. "Okay. I will change the subject. When do we get to see the results of today's little expedition?"

"When we get them back, Matthew and I will sort out the ones we like, and I'll bring them over. Then Megan can choose the one or ones she likes, and we'll get them enlarged."

Matthew and Cameron were delighted when they got the prints back. "These have turned out better than I expected," Matthew remarked. He laughed, "We should go into business."

They selected four, two from each of them and got them enlarged. Matthew had a few school shoots coming up, so he wasn't available during the next few days. Cameron was reluctant to go to Megan's without Matthew, so they took them around one evening.

Megan and her mum spent ages going through the small prints, but in the end, they both agreed that the four that they had got enlarged were the best. At some point during the evening, Mr Chambers joined them and spent a long time going through the small prints and then picked up the enlargements and balanced them against the legs of the coffee table so that they could stand back and admire them. He looked at Megan and smiled, "They've made my lovely daughter look gorgeous."

"Dad, you're making me blush," replied Megan. He turned to Cameron and Matthew.

"You two should go into business together."

Matthew looked at Cameron. "What did I tell you?" and they both laughed.

At the end of the evening, just as they were leaving, Mr Chambers handed Cameron an envelope. "Time is money," he said. "You've spent an afternoon taking the photos. This is just something for your time." They thanked him and left. When they were back at the flat, Cameron opened the envelope. Inside there was £60 and a note. It said, 2 men for 2 hours plus materials and expert knowledge = £60. If you do decide to go into business together, come and see me. I have a lot of contacts who might be useful.

Matthew thought that they should think about it. Cameron wasn't sure. "You're already a professional and are making a good living," he told him. "I'm just an amateur who's had a bit of luck." In the end, Matthew persuaded Cameron to at least think about the possibility of them becoming business partners.

A few days later, Megan rang up. "My friend, Nicki, has seen the photos and wants you to do some of her. You'll love it, Cameron," she told him. "The whole family is into amateur dramatics, and she wants some done in costume. Their house is amazing. Almost all the furniture is Georgian, and a lot of the rooms are decorated in the Georgian style. If you want to do it, I'll take you around and introduce you."

Megan was right. The house was amazing. The rooms looked as though they were straight out of a film set. Matthew and Cameron were given a guided tour by Nicki and her mum and quizzed about what would be the best place to set up for the photos. They came up with some ideas, pointing out which pieces of furniture they would use and the kind of poses they thought would work well, and then her mum dropped a bombshell.

"We would also like some doing of the whole family. We would be in costume too. Do you think that you can do it?" she asked.

Matthew didn't hesitate. "Of course, we can."

Outside, Matthew said, "We need to visit the art gallery. I know that you've been, but it's been a while for me. We need to make a few sketches of these formal poses that you see in these paintings. A bit of research is always a good idea."

When they got the prints back, Cameron and Matthew were delighted with how they had turned out, but their delight was nothing compared to that of Nicki and her parents. They spent a long time selecting the ones that they wanted enlarging and gave instructions that the frames should be gold and highly decorative, just like the ones you'd see around paintings in the art gallery. When they returned with them a week later, the family were ecstatic.

Mr Lansdown said, "These are superb, just what we wanted. You two should set up in business." Later as they were leaving, he handed Matthew an envelope. "I don't know the going rate, but I think that this should cover it." They thanked him and left. Back at the flat, Matthew opened the envelope and counted out £250. After doing a quick calculation, they realised that they had made just over £130.

"Not bad for what was no more than an afternoon's work," said Matthew, "and that's the second time we've been told to go into business together."

Cameron nodded, "Perhaps we should."

It was easy to set up the business. Mr Chambers handled the legal side of everything, including keeping Matthew's school work separate from the partnership. They decided that the business should be called 'MatCam Photography'. There was a small shop unit vacant, next to Matthew's father's luxury car showroom, which they leased as an office and gallery. It also had a room to the rear, which they could use as a studio. However, they hardly ever used it, as much of their work was done on location. It did prove to be ideal, as quite often, some of the customers visiting the car showroom often spent time browsing the gallery, with the result that some of them booked sittings or bought prints.

One thing Matthew was insistent about was weddings. "We definitely should not do weddings," he told Cameron. "They are far too stressful, very tying and no second chances. If we mess up on a portrait sitting, we can always apologise and do it again. You can't do that with a wedding."

Mr Chambers was true to his word in another way. In the early days, he put out recommendations and helped establish the business. Megan and Nicki also put the word out amongst their friends, and soon, the business was thriving. There were times when Matthew was not available because of his school commitments which concerned Cameron slightly, but after the first few occasions, which he managed successfully, it no longer bothered him. What was needed, though, when he was out by himself was an assistant. When he happened to mention it one morning while he was having coffee with Megan, she quickly volunteered to help out, as long as she was free.

The little partnership worked well. Whilst Cameron could worry about the technical details, Megan could demonstrate poses and make suggestions about costumes and makeup. She had studied makeup artistry at college, and that was how she came to be a model at the photographic course. Megan enjoyed these sessions and always talked enthusiastically about them on their way back from a shoot.

Chapter: 41

Megan, Cameron and Matthew got on really well together as they seemed to have a lot in common, so much so that Matthew invited Megan to the club one Saturday when he knew that there was a good live band performing. He introduced her to the group, which was made up mainly of the football and hockey teams, or at least those who had returned after their stints at university. The evening went well. Megan was hardly ever off the dance floor. That was hardly surprising as she was extremely attractive. Cameron noticed that Roy and Alan were especially attentive, and Megan herself persuaded Matthew and Cameron onto the floor at regular intervals during the evening. Meanwhile, Megan and Ruth seemed to quickly form a friendship, and it was Ruth who invited her to come again whenever she liked.

It was during her fourth visit to the club that she brought up the subject of Cameron with Ruth. "You and Cameron are really good friends, aren't you?" She began. "Yes, we are," Ruth replied, "We go back quite a long way now." Megan continued, "I know. It was you and Cameron that saved that little boy's life ages ago, but you are not a couple, are you?"

Ruth shook her head. "If only," she sighed.

Megan looked at her, "So what's the story? Has he got a girlfriend?" she asked.

Ruth immediately understood why Megan was asking. "If you fancy your chances with him, I think that you can forget it. It's a long story," and Ruth proceeded to tell her all about Coral and Cameron. When she had finished, she laughed and said, "I don't think that he's seen her in ages, but if Cameron ever decides he's no longer in love with Coral, you are behind ME in the queue."

The really big break for the business came from Alan's dad. He owned a Spa Hotel on the outskirts of the City. One Saturday evening, he arrived at the club with Alan and went straight to Cameron. He wanted a word with them. Cameron called Matthew across, and Mr Newton took them to one of the side rooms. He explained that he had already seen some of their work at the Lansdown's, and he liked it a lot. He told them that the hotel had been closed for a complete refurbishment, and he wanted a new brochure and asked if they would be interested in taking the photographs for it.

Matthew was quick to respond. "We certainly would, but we have never tried anything like this before, but we'll give it a go." They spent a good while discussing it and agreed to go and look at the hotel the following Monday and then make a decision.

"I like that. It shows common sense. Don't commit until you've had a chance to see what is involved," Mr Newton commented. "See you on Monday," and they shook hands.

As arranged, they visited the hotel on Monday, and Mr Newton gave them a guided tour. They discussed exactly what he had in mind; they made suggestions and made notes. Matthew had invested in a new digital camera, so they took a few test shots and were able to view the results on the rear screen. "When we have got the lighting set up, they will be much better," Matthew told Mr Newton. A few days later, they were back and spent almost the whole day there. Back at the flat, they viewed the images on the computer. They were delighted with the results. One or two needed minor tweaks using software, but on the whole, they were both very happy. They realised that in future, they would both need a digital camera and Cameron purchased one later that week. They never used roll film again after that.

Mr Newton was extremely happy with the results. "I can get the brochure printed now, and I'll make sure that the pictures are credited to you. I'll also put out the word about you. One more thing, if you haven't already got one, you should get a website. Lots of businesses have them now. I can put you in touch with someone to build it for you if you want." They shook hands. "I'll send you a copy of the brochure with Alan when I get them back, and don't forget to invoice me," he smiled, "But I'm sure that you won't!"

They took his advice and using the company that Mr Newton had suggested, they got themselves a website.

A few weeks later, Alan handed them a copy of the brochure. It was passed around their friends amid much admiration. Cameron and Matthew were ecstatic. It was even better than they had hoped for. "Dad says that you can use his recommendation on your website if you want," Alan told them.

Within a few months, their workload had grown considerably. Nicki offered to work part-time in the office to handle enquiries and make bookings. It reached the point where Matthew considered giving up his school contract, but in the end, he decided against it in case the business suddenly failed. They were travelling further and further afield, and no two jobs were the same. They could be shooting the stills for a soap commercial, shooting the guide book for a stately home, shooting family portraits on-site or shooting the interior of a new property development. The work just kept rolling in. They could hardly believe how well it had gone.

Cameron had decided that it was time to get his own place, and he could afford it now. He was very grateful to

Matthew for taking him in when his parents had moved back north. He knew that Matthew was quite happy having him there, but he was conscious that his presence was limiting him, especially as now Matthew and Nicki seemed to be getting on so well.

When Ruth heard that he was starting to look for his own place, she volunteered to go with him to the viewings. He didn't turn her offer down. "A different point of view about a place is always useful," he said. They lost count of the flats that they visited, and he was beginning to think that he would never find the right place when one estate agent suggested that perhaps a small bungalow might suit him, and as it happened, they had one on their books.

Ruth took one look and said that it would be perfect. It was on a quiet estate, had just been modernised and decorated. "What's more?" she said with a smile, "I could easily walk here to visit you." As there was no chain, the deal was done relatively quickly, and Cameron found himself on the property ladder. Ruth helped him choose some furniture and decorative pieces to brighten the place up. She was also true to her word and often walked round to visit him. If the truth be known, he was always happy to see her, as living completely by himself for the first time took some getting used to. He fancied a housewarming and invited his friends from the club. Ruth was a great help with that and acted as if she was the joint host. She even helped clear up after the party was over.

He didn't like the idea of her walking home alone so late at night, and, therefore, he offered to walk her home.

"I could always stay over, Cameron," she smiled.

"That's a good offer, Ruth," he said with a laugh, "but I'm not falling for that one."

She pulled a sulky face. "You can't blame me for trying," she replied. "Okay. Thank you. Walk me home then." However, she did link him all the way home.

With the business thriving and their reputation spreading, both Matthew and Cameron realised that they had differing ideas on the direction the business should take. Matthew, with his school contract, was quite happy to accept fairly local assignments, but they were being approached with assignments by larger and larger companies which occasionally even meant travelling to the continent. Sometimes they were fashion shoots; sometimes, they were shoots for travel companies who were producing new holiday brochures; sometimes, they were product shoots.

Cameron was quite happy to do these, and when she was available, Megan travelled with him. Matthew began to realise that Cameron's assignments were bringing in far more money than his were, and yet they were both earning the same amount of money from the business. One evening he turned up at Cameron's. "We need to talk, Cam," he said. Cameron was a little surprised at what he was proposing.

"It's time to go our separate ways. The assignments that you cover are making far more money than mine, and yet we pay ourselves exactly the same. Don't forget that I also get paid for the school contract. I'm happy just doing the local assignments and fitting them in around my school jobs. That will leave me plenty to survive on. In addition, on the side, I've started doing some sports stuff for the local press, which brings in a bit little bit extra as well. I've no wish to get involved in the big commercials that you are doing. Too much travel for me, especially as Nicki and I are talking about moving in together. The split would be to your benefit. You'd be able to pay yourself more than the company is paying you at the moment."

They discussed it for a while, and in the end, they amicably agreed to separate the business. Later, when he thought about it, Cameron realised that Matthew was right. The work that he did was making far more for the company than the work Matthew did. However, Matthew, because of his school contract, was probably earning a lot more money than he was.

They split the company, and Cameron renamed his new company' CAMMA Imaging', using the first few letters of his Christian and surnames. It didn't make any difference to the amount of work that came in, but the split, as Matthew had hinted it would, put more money in his pocket.

Chapter: 42

Cameron really enjoyed his work. Almost every week was different. His reputation spread, and he was in constant demand. He could be in Milan one week, for the Fashion Week and in Paris a week or two later for their Fashion Week. He could be booked by one of the Sunday Magazines to take fashion shots in Venice and then be in Switzerland a week later to take publicity shots of the latest car produced by one of the top European manufacturers. Sometimes he could be on a beach in Spain shooting swimwear for a sports company.

On some of the fashion shoots, much to Ruth's dismay, he took Megan with him as his 'make-up artist', as by now she was fully qualified. The arrangement worked both ways. He knew that he could trust her to do a good job, and her association with him led to her getting well known in the profession, and she started getting assignments with other photographers.

It was this variety of assignments that meant that he was never bored. Often these assignments presented him with new challenges that he enjoyed solving. Where ever the job was, though, he usually drove there. His little Corsa was a thing of the past. He now drove a BMW X5 because he needed the space in the back to store all his equipment.

He had flown to a job once with just his camera kit, having been assured by the client that the lighting equipment that he needed would be available. When he arrived, the equipment that they had provided wasn't up to the specifications that he had asked for, and they wasted several valuable hours whilst the correct equipment was sourced and hired. He vowed never to fall for that again.

Just after lunchtime in London, the day after he had met Penny in Brussels, he had completed the stills for the shampoo commercial and having nothing booked for the next few days, he took her advice and drove north to the Big House. It had been a while since he'd seen his parents, and he knew that they would be pleased to see him. He arrived there in the late afternoon. His mum opened the door, and a big smile crossed her face.

"Hello, love. This is unexpected. You should have phoned."

"It was a sort of impulse. I've nothing booked for a few days, so a trip up here to see you and relax a little seemed like a good idea. Is dad in?"

"No, but he won't be long."

"And Uncle Ben?"

"He's probably asleep. He takes a nap in the afternoon these days." "I'll go and see him later."

It wasn't long before his dad turned up, and they sat chatting, mostly about Cameron's work and the life that he was leading.

"It's not as glamorous as you might think. Travel gets tiring. Two days ago, I was in Brussels. So it's good to take a break. The Brussels job paid extremely well, so I can't complain. It's one of the best accounts that I have got. There was one surprise in Brussels, though. I met Penny. You remember her." They nodded, and he told them all about the chance meeting, but leaving out Penny's instructions to go and find Coral.

After a meal, he went to visit Uncle Ben in the 'Uncle Flat'. It was a while since Cameron had seen him, and whilst he looked older, it was obvious that he had lost none of his sparkle. They talked for a while. Ben was really interested in Cameron's work and remarked that it was clever of Cameron to see different parts of the world at other people's expense.

Then he looked Cameron straight in the eye. "Cameron, there is one thing about you that disappoints me. Whatever has happened to Coral? I remember telling you to look after her the first time she came here. Have you found someone else because if you have, she must be a remarkable woman?"

"No, Uncle, I haven't found anyone else. There have been a few good friends, but none have them have ever replaced her."

"So, my boy, you still love her."

He didn't hesitate, "Yes."

"Well, what are you going to do about it? Go and get her back."

"Uncle, she might have found someone else by now. She might be married with children."

"She might, Cameron, but I'd be surprised if she were."

Cameron looked puzzled. "Why do you say that?"

"Because that first time we met and I took her into the kitchen, and we talked. I asked her what she wanted in life. Do you know what she said?" Cameron shook his head. "To be a vet and to marry you, and it didn't matter in which order it happened."

"But that was years ago. Things change, people change."

"True, very true," replied his uncle, "But something about that young lady tells me that she meant what she said. If you want my advice, you need to go back there and at least find out what has happened to her. If you don't, you will regret it for the rest of your life. I told you she was a diamond. Diamonds are worth looking after. Make sure that you go. Go tomorrow."

Cameron sat for a moment, all sorts of memories flashing through his mind. Then he realised Ben was right. He would go tomorrow. When he was back with his parents in the main house, his dad asked, "How was he?"

"Same as usual. Bright as a button, and right as usual. He told me that I should go back home and try and find out about Coral. He thinks that she will still be waiting for me, and do you know what? I hope that she is!"

His mum looked at him. "Cameron love, so do I, so do I."

In bed that night, he thought about the last few days. He knew that he still loved Coral, even after all this time, even though he couldn't remember the last time he had seen her or even spoken to her. Now in the space of a few days, two people had told him to go and find her. What's more, they were both convinced that she would still be single. As he lay there, he began to fill with optimism. He would get across there tomorrow and find out if Penny and Uncle Ben were right.

Chapter: 43

Everything seemed to be much the same as it was when he left all those years ago. Here was the primary school they all went to, and as he turned left off the main road and drove past the school playground, he could see the playing fields on the right where once upon a time they played football on a Saturday morning. He smiled to himself as he remembered that the girls loyally used to come and support them even when it was proverbial brass monkey weather. The children's playground was still there, too, with its few swings, a slide and a seesaw. Driving on, the little parade of shops was still there. One was still a hairdressing salon, another was now a convenience store, and even the sweet shop appeared to be still there.

Micky was an old fashioned shopkeeper who could be a bit grumpy but would even pour out an ounce of sweets from the jars if that's all you could afford, as long as you said please. Then he would tip them off the scale pan into a white paper bag which he fastened by holding the two top corners and then swinging the bag over the top.

Now he signalled left and turned into the street where he used to live. His old house was a bit more than halfway up on the left—number 27. You could get into the street from both ends.

He pulled up outside. It looked very much the same. It had some new windows, perhaps, and definitely a new door. The gate had gone, and the wall cut back to get a car, or maybe two, onto the drive. He got out of the car. He didn't know why. He could see the house perfectly well from the driver's seat. Nostalgia, probably. He leaned against the passenger door and wallowed in the memories of his past. He tried to recall the last time that he'd been here. He realised that it must have been the Christmas that he'd spent at the Brownes, and that was in his second year at university. That made it at least six years ago or maybe more.

He had sort of lost track of time when a voice asked, "Can I help you? You have been staring at my house for the last ten minutes."

He stood up straight, and in front of him, in the garden, was a very pleasant looking woman who he guessed was in her late forties.

"I'm terribly sorry. I used to live here once, with my mum and dad. I was in the area, so I thought I'd come back and take a look. I've got lots of happy memories of this street. It's the first time in ages that I've been back. I'm sorry if you thought I was being intrusive. I'll go now."

"No, don't go." She paused as if thinking then, "Your surname doesn't happen to be Mason, does it? Only we bought the house off Mr & Mrs Mason."

"It is. I am Cameron, their son."

"Well, Cameron, it's very nice to meet you after all this time. We heard quite a lot about you after we first moved in. Have you time for a cup of tea?"

"That's kind if it's not too much trouble, and you've got me wondering now what you heard about me."

Inside, he sat at the table whilst she brewed up. He looked around. Apart from the decorations and the furniture, nothing much had changed. Through the kitchen door, he could see that the kitchen had new contemporary fittings. They looked almost brand new. When he lived here, the house had two rooms downstairs. Now it had one big one. The dividing wall had been taken out and replaced with sliding doors. The doors were open now, and he could see through to the street.

As she emerged from the kitchen carrying a tray with two ornate mugs on and a plate with a few biscuits, he said, "I'm sorry I can't remember the name of the family we sold the house to."

"We are The Dawsons, but you can call me Ellen. My husband is Robert, and my son is Luke. I think that you've met him once or twice."

Cameron nodded, "Yes, I think I have."

She started to pour the tea and then passed the mug to him.

"There's sugar if you want it and more milk."

He took a sip and then, "I'm intrigued. What did you hear about me and who from?"

"Mostly from the Brownes up the road. I believe you knew them well."

"I did, very well. Do they still live there?"

"They do, and from what I know about you, from them, they would be delighted to see you. Especially Coral."

He looked shocked. "Coral! Does she still live with her mum and dad?"

"No, but she often visits. If there is a little blue car outside, she'll be there now."

"I don't think there is. When I pulled up, mine was the only car parked on the road between here and Holly Street."

"What a pity," She smiled and pointedly looked at his left hand. "I see that you don't have a wedding ring." He shook his head.

"Neither does she." She smiled again.

There was a pause. "Are you telling me that Coral is not married?" She nodded.

"But how do you know about our past? It was a long time ago."

"When we first moved in, Luke found it hard at school and even harder to make friends."

"Tell me about it," he muttered.

She glanced at him, slightly puzzled, but continued, "It was Coral who came to his rescue. She invited him to the youth club. She introduced him to everyone and told them that he was living in your old house. They were all really friendly towards him, and at last, he began to enjoy things again. He really liked Coral. After all, she was and still is a pretty girl. He tried asking her out several times. But she always refused.

She'd go out with him as a friend, she told him, but he could never be her boyfriend." He asked her, "Why not?" "It was because of you. She told him that she loved you. Eventually, he gave that one up and accepted her as a friend. They are still friends now. Jenny had told Coral that she liked Luke a lot. Coral persuaded Luke to ask Jenny out instead. I'm glad she did. Luke and Jenny are married now, and I have a lovely little grandson."

She looked out of the window and then, with a knowing smile, said. "I think that it might be a good idea if you left now and went and paid the Browne's a visit. I've just seen a little blue car drive past."

He didn't move, "Go on, you will regret it for the rest of your life if you don't. I know you still love her. I could see it in your eyes when I said she wasn't married. Go on, GO. Not many people get second chances. GO."

He got up. "Thank you for the tea, and I may be back later to thank you again."

She saw him to the door and watched him walk up the street before he paused briefly at the drive before walking to the front door.

As he walked towards number 15, all sorts of things were going through his mind as he tried to digest everything he had learnt in the last half an hour. What worried him most was how would he be received? Was everything Mrs Dawson told him true? He paused for a few seconds.

He rang the bell and held his breath, heard noises on the other side and then the door opened. There was Mrs Browne. For a split second, she looked stunned. Then she smiled, "Hello, love. What a nice surprise. It's lovely to see you after all this time, and I know someone who'll be even more pleased,"

She turned and shouted up the stairs, "Coral love, somebody to see you,"

He heard steps on the stairs, and then there she was. As pretty as ever, slightly older, of course, but she had hardly changed at all and in that split second, he knew. He still loved her, not still loved her, but had always loved her.

She stopped short when she saw him. A look of complete astonishment flashed across her face. "Cameron."

They stood looking at each other for a few seconds, then he said, "I always told you that I would come back for you. I hope it's not too late."

She almost flew out of the door and flung her arms around him. "Just hold me, Cameron, just hold me like you used to do."

And he did. He held her tight, and it was as if they were back as teenagers. She looked up at him, and he kissed her. "I was first with the kiss this time," he smiled, and she kissed him back.

"When you two have finished making a complete exhibition of yourselves on the doorstep you'd better come in."

"Okay, Mrs Browne." Coral looked at him, he nodded, and hand in hand, they went in.

Later, when both life stories had been told, they went for a walk by the canal and stopped under the bridge.

"Do you remember the first time we came here together," he asked.

"Of course I do, and I remember what we said as well."

"What did we say?"

"You said, 'shall we try it again?' I said, 'what? The holding or the kissing' and you said 'both', so we did."

He laughed and said, "Shall we try it again?"

"What the holding or the kissing?"

"Both", so they did and again and again and maybe again.

When they got back to the Browne's, he said that he'd better be off.

Coral looked at her mum. "Mum, I've only just got him back. Kidnap him, please."

Mrs Browne pulled a face, "I'm not sure that's legal." She looked at her husband, who nodded, "but if you want to stay, you are more than welcome, Cameron."

"That's settled then," Coral announced, and she cuddled closer to him on the sofa.

"I think I'd better go and move my car from lower down the road."

Mr Browne didn't often say much, but now he spoke. "That rather nice motor is yours, is it? Very nice. Just park it across the drive. Coral's off for a few days, and I'm not going out tomorrow."

"I'm coming with you to get it. I'm not letting you out of my sight again." Just as they reached his car, they met Mr & Mrs Dawson coming the other way.

"I told you," she said, looking at Cameron. "Now, don't lose her again."

"No, Mrs Dawson, I won't and thank you."

Coral hugged Mrs Dawson, "Thank you for making him ring our bell. Thank you so much."

When the car was parked, they went back inside.

Mrs Browne was first to speak. "So, where is Cameron sleeping tonight? Should I make up the spare room?" She was smiling.

"Mum, I've told you, I've only just got him back, and I'm not letting him out of my sight. He's sleeping in my room."

Mrs Browne looked at Cameron, "Well, what have you got to say about it?" Her smile was even wider now.

"I'll sleep where I'm told," he replied.

"That's settled then. You're sleeping in my room." She looked at her mum and went on, "I'm a big girl now."

"It's okay, Coral, love. While you were sorting the car out, your dad and I had already spoken about it. We knew what you would say. So now it's up to Cameron." She looked at him. "What do you say?"

"If you are sure that you don't mind, I'll share with Coral. We've still got lots to talk about."

"That's fine with us, Cameron, but people don't usually go to bed to talk," she laughed.

"MUM, what are you suggesting?"

Chapter: 44

Later, in Coral's room, he was surprised. On the few previous visits he had made to the Browne's, he had never been in Coral's bedroom. He'd always used the spare room. On the bedside table in a silver frame was the photo of them kissing on their last night together at the Youth Club. On a little corner shelf was his 'Player of the Season' award. On her pillow was the little teddy he had given her on the morning he left. She saw him looking at it. "He always sleeps there," she said. "Look in the tin." In the tin was £80 in ten-pound notes. "That's the money your uncle gave us. We said that we'd save it and spend it on ourselves. Do you remember?"

He nodded, "I remember."

On the walls, there were photo frames that had multiple apertures and in each aperture was a photo of them together or him by himself that had been taken on the French Holiday. Right in the middle was the one of him asleep on the ferry. She saw him looking at those as well.

"Cameron, that holiday was the happiest I've ever been, until tonight, and look." She reached inside the neck of her blouse and lifted out the locket he had given her the night before he left. "Except when I am at work, I never take it off." Then she held her right hand out to him. "Look. The Claddagh ring."

He said. "I noticed it when we kissed on the doorstep."

She looked him straight in the eye, "Cameron, I've hardly ever taken it off, and I wore it all the time in Edinburgh."

When he returned from the bathroom, she was already in bed. He got in, and they snuggled up. For a while, they talked in whispers about things they had done and not mentioned earlier. Then she said, "Cameron, just hold me tonight, please. We've waited so long. A bit longer won't make any difference." He said nothing but just held her tight.

After a while, he said, "Coral, are you asleep?"

"No, but nearly."

"Can I ask you something, Coral Browne?"

"Yes, go on."

"Will you marry me?"

She shot up. "Cameron Mason, you've already asked me to marry you once. Remember?"

"I remember."

"And what did I say?"

"Yes, Yes, Yes."

"Well, I haven't changed my mind, so it's still Yes, Yes, Yes," and she kissed him. "Now go to sleep."

In the morning, they were up quite early, much to Mrs Browne's surprise. "Couldn't you sleep?" she asked. Mr Browne looked up from his paper. "What?" she said, smiling.

"We slept very well, thank you," Coral replied, "and that's all you need to know. We've got things to do, so we're off into town."

They helped tidy the breakfast things away, said goodbye and set off down the road hand in hand. Mrs Browne watched them go. "I think I know what those two are up to," She said to no one in particular.

"So do I," said Mr Browne, "but lets' see, shall we? No good jumping the gun."

In town, they went window shopping until they found what they were looking for in an upmarket jewellery shop.

In one tray, in particular, there were several rings that Coral liked the look of. They went inside, and Coral spent some time trying on rings until she found one that she really liked and was in her size. She smiled up at Cameron, "This one please."

Cameron was pleased. It wasn't too showy, and it had a modest-sized blue sapphire in the middle surrounded on either side by a small diamond.

"Is madam going to wear it now, or would you like it boxing and wrapping."

"I'll wear it now, but I would like the box, please."

"Certainly, madam and I hope that you'll both be very happy," With the transaction complete and Uncle Ben's £80 paying part of it, they went and found somewhere to have a celebration lunch.

Coral couldn't wait to get back home. Once through the door, she dashed to her mum.

"Look, mum!" and she waved her left hand at her. Her mum got hold of the waving hand to get a closer look.

"It's gorgeous, Coral." She stepped away and looked at Cameron. "Is it alright to give you a hug?" She didn't wait for the answer. She hugged him anyway. "Cameron, you don't know how pleased I am."

By this time, Mr Browne had arrived. "Somebody looks very happy," he said, hugging his daughter, "and I can see that you are as well," he said, turning to Cameron and shaking his hand.

"Well, I suppose that I'll have to pay for a wedding now. It's a good job that I've had a good few years to save up for it," he said good-naturedly. "Let's all sit down and have a celebration drink. We guessed that this might happen today, so after you went out this morning, we went out and bought something to celebrate with. Good job, we guessed right, or it might have been wasted…or maybe not. It's good stuff."

Later, when they were alone in the other room, Coral said, "Cameron, you do love me, don't you, because it's been years since we've seen each other, and we've got engaged in less than 24 hours since meeting up again."

He turned and looked her straight in the eyes, "Coral Browne, I've been in love with you ever since the night of Gordon's accident. I think that I was probably in love with you even before that. Like when I came to your party, or maybe even before that when we were in primary school together, and we used to walk to school together with our mums or play in the garden together, I just didn't realise that it was love at the time. I can't believe that I was stupid enough to almost lose you. You were always there. Yes, yes, yes. I do really love you." And he kissed her long and hard.

Later before they went to bed, he said, "Tomorrow, we better go and see my mum and dad and show off the ring."

"But they live miles away. We can't get there and come back in a day."

"We can get there in less than half a day now," he replied. "You remember Uncle Ben." She nodded. "He's very old now and needs a bit of looking after. He signed the Big House over to mum and dad and had a granny flat built at the side of the house, all on one level. Well, an uncle flat actually, and he moved in there. Mum and dad sold up when they came back from France and moved into the main house whilst I was in my last year at Exeter. So we can go and see them tomorrow. That's if you've nothing better to do."

Chapter: 45

Next day, they were up early-ish and off to the seaside. He was already in the car when just as she was about to get in, Coral spotted Mrs Dawson coming towards them. Coral waited for her.

"Look, Mrs Dawson."

"Well, that didn't take long dear. I'm so happy for you both." She gave Cameron the thumbs up. "I'll tell Jenny. The word will soon get around."

The trip to the Big House didn't take much more than an hour. "Cameron, I'm nervous. I've not seen your mum and dad in ages. What will they think?"

"They will be pleased to see you, and it will be like we've never been apart." When they pulled up on the drive, she leaned across and kissed him.

"Cameron, I'm so happy."

"So am I." He looked her straight in the eyes and whispered, "And I Love Her."

She whispered back, "And I Love Him." They got out of the car, and before they had a chance to ring the bell, the door opened. Mrs Mason took one look at Coral and flung her arms around her.

"Coral" was all she said and then kissed her on the cheek. By this time, his dad had appeared.

"Looks like you found her then. It's lovely to see you, Coral."

Mrs Mason stepped back and took hold of both Coral's hands. "Let me have a good look at you, love." It was then she noticed the ring. She looked at Cameron and then back at Coral. They were both smiling.

"Yes, mum. We're engaged."

His dad was first to react and shook Cameron's hand. "Congratulations, son, what took you so long? It should have happened years ago. Can I kiss you, Coral?" She nodded happily.

Then Mrs Mason kissed Coral again. "Coral, I'm so happy for you. He's right. I can't really understand why you drifted apart."

"Let' not talk about that," said Cameron, "Is there any lunch?"

After lunch, Coral filled his parents in with things that had happened since they last met. Cameron said that they had better go and see Uncle Ben. They knocked on his door and waited. Eventually, it opened. Uncle Ben took one look at Coral, and his eyes lit up. "Come in, come in. I see that you took my advice Cameron and it was obviously worth it. You can't know, Coral, how happy I am to see you."

She smiled, "And I'm very happy to see you," she replied. When they were sitting down, he said, "I told him to go and find you, you know, but he was scared that you might have found someone else."

Coral looked at Cameron and shook her head. "There's never ever ever been anyone else," she replied.

"That's what I told him. The first time we met, you told me that you only wanted two things in life: to marry Cameron and be a vet. Do you remember?"

She nodded, "I remember."

He continued, "I suppose the vet bit came first then." She nodded again. "What about the second bit?" They both smiled, and she held up her hand for him to see. "That's excellent news," he grinned, "And I can tell that you are both very happy. Come and give an old man a hug, and then tell me about life as a vet."

When she had finished, he said, "Where do you live, Coral?"

"When I'm on duty, I have a small flat near the park. When I'm not on duty, I usually go and stay at home. I'll be back at work the day after tomorrow."

"What will the arrangements be when you are married?" he inquired. "We haven't thought that far ahead, Uncle," Cameron replied.

"Well, when you have, you'd better come and see me. Houses are expensive, you know, and well, who else do I have to spend my money on?" They looked at each other

"Uncle Ben, are you offering to buy us a house?" Cameron asked.

"I most certainly am."

"That's very kind," Coral whispered, "Are you sure?"

"Certainly, and by the way, I've just remembered something. What did you spend that money on that I gave you both all those years ago?"

"We saved it, and in the end, it helped pay for the ring," answered Cameron.

"You saved it all this time! Who looked after it?"

Coral replied, "I did. I put it in a tin on a shelf in my bedroom. The only time I touched it was when the new notes came out, and I got them changed at the bank."

"I meant you to spend it almost immediately: but I suppose that it's been put to good use now," he laughed.

Back in the Big House, they sat and talked with his parents. Coral was squeezed up to Cameron on the sofa, her head resting on his shoulder. Cameron told them about Uncle Ben's offer.

"You should accept it," his dad said, "He can easily afford it. Believe me. He won't even miss the money. He thinks of you as the grandson he never had. Now, changing the subject, what are you two going to do now? Are you having something to eat now and driving back tonight, or shall we go and eat out later, a sort of celebration?" "That would be lovely," Coral replied. His mum chimed in, "I've made up the spare room, just in case you decide to stay over." She looked at them knowingly.

"That's great, mum, but we haven't brought an overnight case." She looked disappointed.

Coral spoke up, "We won't need much. We've got a bit of time to go and buy toothbrushes and a few other things before the shops close."

Later they went to a restaurant that his parents often used. Mr Mason proposed a toast to the pair of them and wished them happiness. Cameron thought that he'd never heard his dad speak like that before.

"Thanks, Dad." When they were in bed, Cameron whispered to her, "This has been a good day and full of surprises. Are you happy?" "Yes, yes, yes." She kissed him. "Your Uncle is so generous. Are we going to accept his offer?"

"We will probably have to, or he may never speak to us again," Cameron whispered. "But we need to think about it carefully. I don't want to buy a house that I wouldn't be able to afford, just because I have a rich uncle offering to buy it."

Mrs Dawson was as good as her word. Once Jenny knew that Coral and Cameron were back together, she was anxious to get round to see Coral. She had to wait until she was sure that Coral was at home, but when she received a phone call from her mother in law, telling her that the little blue car was at the Browne's, she wasted no time in getting there. Coral opened the door.

"Is it true, Coral? Are you back together? Are you engaged?" Coral just waved her left hand in front of Jenny's face. The smile on Coral's face just said it all. They hugged each other.

"Oh, Coral, I'm so happy for you." They sat and talked for ages, during which time Jenny was hatching a plan. She kept it to herself, but an engagement party with everyone back together seemed like a good idea.

She put her plan into action. When Coral was back at work, she visited the Browne's again and told them of her intentions. She needed Mrs Browne to give her Coral's shift pattern and to find out when Cameron would be available. Mrs Browne was keen to be involved and promised to keep it a secret. Once Jenny had those details, she needed a venue that was available at fairly short notice. After a few dead ends, she managed to book the Canalside Cricket Club Function room and their in-house caterers. Then the invitations went out, stressing to everyone that the party was to be a surprise. Mr and Mrs Mason had to be involved as well, and at their suggestion, some invitations went to some of Cameron's friends in Bristol.

The party was a huge success. The secret had been well kept. The night before, Coral and Cameron were staying at the Browne's. Mr Browne casually mentioned that the function room at the cricket club had been refurbished, so if it was alright with them, he had booked a table for four for the following evening. "A sort of celebration," he said. "That's a lovely idea, dad. Thank you."

Mr Browne drove them to the club and carefully engineered it so that Coral and Cameron went in ahead of him and Mrs Browne. As they went through the door, they were stopped dead in their tracks. The room was decorated with helium balloons and streamers with 'congratulations' written on them, and they were greeted by a sea of smiling faces and a round of applause. Before they could recover from the shock, they were buried in a wave of hugs, kisses and handshakes.

Coral turned to her dad, "Did you sort this?"

He shook his head and pointed to Jenny. "She arranged everything." Jenny was smiling at them. Coral went across and gave her a big hug. Cameron spotted his mum and dad and went over to them.

"You knew about this as well." His mum smiled.

"Yes, love, we did and isn't it nice to see everyone again." He nodded. "It is, it's great. Then he noticed Ruth, Gary and Susanna, Matthew and Nicki. He went across to them and made sure that they were introduced to their old friends.

A lot of the time was spent catching up. Ian and Pam were married, Tony and Kate were living together, and Gordon introduced them to Olivia, his ice skating partner and girlfriend.

Jenny introduced Cameron to Luke. "This is Luke, but I think that you met him one Friday night at the Browne's."

"I remember," Cameron replied, "but it was a long time ago." There wasn't much dancing early in the evening, but after the buffet, the dance floor was hardly ever deserted. At one point, Ian asked for quiet.

"Way, way back," he began, "and it seems like many centuries ago," and everyone laughed, "We put on a performance of 'Joseph'. At the time, we were pleasantly surprised to find that one of us had a superb voice. Tonight, James is going to sing for us again, accompanied by Tony." James climbed onto the stage. There was applause and cheering.

"We have discovered that there is one song that is special for Coral and Cameron," he announced, "and I am delighted to sing it for them, and I hope that they like it and will take to the floor."

Coral looked at Cameron. With a puzzled look on his face, he shook his head. As the first few notes were played and James began to sing 'And I love her,' it dawned on both of them at the same time. She pulled Cameron onto the floor. With their arms around each other, they swayed gently to the music, and as the song finished, just as he did all those years before, he mouthed 'And I love her', and then they kissed.

The moment was broken by loud applause, cheering and whistling. They went to James. Coral hugged him. "Thank you, James, that was lovely, but how did you know?"

"I was told," he replied, but Cameron had worked it out. There were only a few other people present who saw it the first time, but he guessed that it was his mum and dad.

Then they were joined on the dance floor by all their friends and as the evening progressed Cameron was really pleased to see that Ruth and James were spending a lot of time together and he mentioned it to Coral.

"They're two nice people," she replied, "Let's hope that it works out for them."

At the end of the evening, Cameron made a little speech.

"Most of you know that I don't make speeches," and here there was laughter, "but we would just like to thank Jenny for organising this evening. It was a complete surprise to us. Thank you all for coming. It was lovely to see all our old friends, and we hope to see you all again at the wedding."

It took a little while for everyone to disperse. No one really wanted the evening to end, but at last, they were left with just their parents. The secret had been so well kept that they didn't know that his mum and dad were going to spend the night at the Browne's.

"Whose car are you going to ride back in?" his dad asked. They looked at each other.

"I think that we'll walk back," Cameron replied.

So once again, they found themselves under the canal bridge. Cameron held her close and said, "Shall we do it again?"

She smiled, "What, the holding or the kissing?" But she already knew the answer, so they did for quite a long time.

Chapter: 46

Cameron was well aware that he would have to relocate, as he knew there was no way Coral would leave her job at the Safari Park, nor would he want her to. He started to look for office space close to the park. He didn't need a great deal of space anymore, and he certainly no longer needed a large studio. Most of the commercial shoots were now done in fully-equipped professional studios or on location. As he was away quite a lot of the time, he enlisted the help of his parents to visit a few industrial estates and draw up a list of possibilities. Finally, after visiting some of them, he plumped for an estate in a semi-rural location with not more than a dozen units. He chose one of the smaller units with a front office and a reasonably sized conference room to the rear, which could double as a studio if necessary. In addition, he put his bungalow in Bristol on the market and started living with his parents.

When they managed to get time together, Cameron and Coral visited estate agents looking for a house. Coral's parents were keen to be involved in the house hunting and visited quite a few properties and made a list of several that they thought might appeal to the couple. However, it was Coral that eventually found what they were looking for in a small village not more than 10 miles from the safari park.

On the way back to her parent's after one shift, she made a slight detour through the village. She spotted the 'For Sale' sign and immediately liked the look of it. She made an appointment to view, liked what she saw and got in touch with Cameron, who was working up in Scotland but would be back two days later. She was convinced that he would like it and was worried that it might get snapped up before he could see it.

As soon as he saw it, he knew that this was the place for them, and they put in an offer that was accepted. Cameron knew that they should tell his uncle that they were buying a house, so one evening he collected Coral, and they went to see Uncle Ben. He was delighted to see them.

They showed him pictures that they had taken of the house and told him all about it.

"I can see that you are really taken with it so like I promised, I will help you to buy it. What was the asking price?" They told him.

"But we put an offer in that was less than that, and it was accepted," Cameron explained. Uncle Ben stood up and went to his cabinet, opened a drawer, took out his cheque book and wrote out a cheque. He gave it to Cameron. A look of surprise crossed his face, and he passed it to Coral. It was a lot more than the asking price. Coral was the first to speak, "Uncle Ben, that's far too much; we can't take that."

He smiled at her, wagged his finger at her and said, "You just take it. The excess will help to furnish it, and before either of you say another word, don't argue with me."

Coral got up, kissed him on the cheek and hugged him. "Thank you, thank you," she whispered in his ear.

Chapter: 47

Cameron was nervous. He fiddled with his watch. He kept checking the time. "Relax, man," Ian, his best man, urged. "She'll be here and on time. You needn't worry about that. Coral has been waiting for this since the first day you played in the sandpit with her at infant school." Cameron smiled at that. That could be true, he thought.

"You mark my words," Ian went on, "as soon as that clock starts to chime 2 o'clock, she WILL be here."

Twenty seconds later, the clock did start to chime. A few seconds later, the vicar stood up and nodded to them. "She's here," he whispered."

Ian turned to Cameron. "See. What did I tell you?" and they stood up and moved to the centre of the aisle. They both turned to watch Coral enter the church. Out of the corner of his eye, Cameron saw Coral's mum smiling at him. "At last," she mouthed, and he smiled.

He watched her walk down the aisle linked to her dad. Cameron thought that she was more beautiful than he had ever seen her. She was smiling all the way, and her eyes were fixed on him. She reached the front, still looking at him. Mr Browne unlinked himself and went and sat with his wife, who was looking on proudly. Coral turned and handed her bouquet to Jenny, then Jenny and Lorna went and took their seats. The rest of the ceremony was a bit of a blur to Cameron. He remembered looking into Coral's eyes as he said, "I do," and he knew that he said it with great certainty. He remembered Coral looking at him intently as she said, "I do," quietly almost as if it was to him only.

He remembered the vicar saying, "I now pronounce you man and wife. You may kiss the bride." He did. He remembered the laughter when the vicar said, "I think that's enough for now." He remembered the sea of faces as they walked down the church aisle. He couldn't tell you who he shook hands with outside or who wished both of them luck. He remembered Mrs Browne smiling and kissing him on the cheek before whispering, "I always knew, you know." He did see his mum and dad hugging and kissing Coral.

There was Penny. He went and kissed her on the cheek. He smiled at her, "Thank you for the best bit of advice ever."

Then he spotted Ruth. She was holding hands with James. They seemed to be very close. He went across to them.

"You two seem happy," he said. Ruth smiled. "We are," she replied. "We're really glad that I got invited to your engagement party."

He knew that lots of photographs were taken with lots of friends and relations. The only one that he was one hundred per cent sure was taken was the one with 'The Gang'.

The other thing that he was sure of was that he was married to Coral, and that was the best feeling he had ever had.

She stood at the back of the church with her dad. She saw everyone turn to look at her as the organ began playing. If she could, she was going to remember everything about this day. She had thought about it, wished for it even, for as long as she could remember. She could see Cameron at the front, watching her as she walked steadily towards him, her eyes fixed on him. She knew she was smiling and, at the same time, almost crying with happiness.

She remembered them repeating the vows. She remembered Cameron saying "I do." and could tell he really meant it. She remembered saying "I do" to Cameron as though he was the only one there, and she remembered them putting the rings on each other's fingers.

She remembered the vicar saying, "I now pronounce you man and wife." She remembered that their kiss went on a bit too long and that everyone laughed when the vicar said, "I think that's enough for now." She remembered the walk out of the church with everyone smiling at them. She remembered the big hug she got from her mum, who whispered in her ear," Happy now, love?" "Yes, mum, very happy." She remembered the kiss she got from her dad. He didn't do that very often!

She saw Penny in amongst his friends from Bristol and went and hugged her. "Thank you for making him come back for me," she whispered. She remembered the hugs and kisses she got from Cameron's mum and dad. She remembered all the photographs, especially the one with 'The Gang'.

She remembered the best bit of all. She was now Cameron's wife. At last, she was Mrs Coral Mason.

Later, at the reception, the happy couple took to the floor for the first dance. The chosen song could only be 'And I love her.'